Tempting Fate

VANESSA E. KELMAN

WORD COLLAGE PUBLISHING

Chapter 1

OCTOBER

Jackie hated change. Actually, hate was a strong word. It was more like she was terrified of change. That's not to say that nothing had ever changed for her. Just that the changes were usually out of her control. Like today.

The letter was professional, concise. She sat at her kitchen table reading it over and over. The doctor she worked for, a pediatrician, was retiring. Understandable, considering he was well into his seventies. But it meant that either he would be selling his practice or the office would be closing. The decision had still not been made. And either option made Jackie panic.

With a deep breath, Jackie tried to fortify herself. *This would be good*, she told herself. Maybe this change would encourage her to make other changes in her life at last. Maybe she could get off her hamster wheel and join "real life," whatever that was. A year ago she had asked a fellow book club member, Mary, about making some changes. Mary had revitalized her life, and Jackie hoped to do the same. But it was easy to talk about it. It was a lot harder to actually take the steps. So, aside from some volunteer work around the holidays, nothing had been different. And it remained the same to this day.

Forcing herself to take a few deep breaths, Jackie stood up and made a cup of tea. As she stirred in the sugar, her mind whirred. She wished she could be excited about the change. Her life had grown quite stagnant. She got up, went to work, came home. Tuesday nights were book club meetings, but the rest of the week was spent at home, cleaning or quietly reading on her own. She had a few friends she met for coffee on occasion, but their lives were so different from her own that she found they didn't have much to talk about. She should be happy that things were getting shaken up.

This would be good. But she couldn't help biting her lower lip in worry.

Paul took a deep breath and slammed the trunk of his car. *This will be good*, he told himself. A change of scenery, a bit of a break from norm. Maybe his wife would come to her senses while he was gone. Divorce? It seemed so official, so final. And he loved her. Didn't he?

After a quick mental checklist, Paul slid into the driver's seat and inserted his key into the ignition. He wasn't thrilled to be leaving, but Pam hadn't given him many options. Leave of his own free will, or she would have all of his items on the curb when he returned from work. Who would have thought she could be so harsh?

At least Uncle Bill had been willing to take him in. Paul had always been close with his uncle, but as the years had passed, they didn't see each other as often as they liked. This time should give them an opportunity to catch up, and maybe Paul could get a little advice on what the heck had gone wrong.

It took an hour to get to Bill's house, but it was a scenic drive. As Paul pulled into the driveway of the modest suburban home, he took another deep breath. This would be good. A couple of weeks away from work, a couple of weeks away from Pam. It would be a great time to determine his next steps. Would it be enough time to convince Pam? He could only hope.

Chapter 2

She loved her mother. Jackie had to keep telling herself that. As trying as it could be to carry on a conversation with her, Jackie loved her. "Hi, Mom!" She forced enthusiasm into her voice.

"Good morning, Jacqueline. How are you?"

"I'm fine."

Pleasantries and small talk followed, and by the time Jackie hung up the phone fifteen minutes later, she was exhausted. Her mother insisted on these conversations once a week, but it was difficult to find enough to fill them. No matter what she said, she knew her mother would be opinionated and judgmental – which was perhaps why she had held off so long to change in the first place. There was always the little voice in the back of her head asking "what would Mother say?"

Between the conversation with her mother and the aftermath of her boss's letter, Jackie felt like hiding in the corner and sulking like a child. And the combination left Jackie in no mood to return to work on Monday. But she had little choice. There were still bills to pay, and it certainly wouldn't show her maturity to hide in the corner and sulk like a child. Though if she would be out of a job anyway, it probably didn't matter much.

It was a typical Monday morning, with the phones ringing off the hook and a line of patients waiting to be seen. It was the beginning of flu season, and the sick children waiting in the front room broke Jackie's heart. She loved the little darlings – it was one of her favorite parts of the job – but she hated seeing them so miserable.

Around noon traffic slowed for a bit, since that was when Dr. Collins and the staff usually took their lunch break. Jackie set the phone to go into voice mail and reached for her lunch bag. The bell on the front door, though, caused her to look up. An attractive man in his late thirties smiled at her. There was no child by his side, and Jackie thought perhaps he was lost.

"Can I help you?"

"Actually I was looking for my uncle. I wanted to take him to lunch. Is Bill in?"

"Let me check. Have a seat." Jackie gestured to the waiting room and sat back down. She rang the doctor's private office extension. When he picked up, she explained the visitor, then turned to the man waiting. "He'll be right up."

"Thanks."

Jackie resumed her tasks, then retreated to the lunch room. Dr. Collins never discussed family. He had never so much as mentioned any siblings or children. Jackie knew he had been married once, but his wife had passed away nearly twenty years earlier, and to the best of Jackie's knowledge, he had never sought companionship after that. She supposed that once you found the person you were meant to love forever, replacing that person would be impossible. She sighed wistfully, then scolded herself. She had been reading too many romance novels. Still, it was nice to know the doctor wasn't completely alone.

Just as Jackie was returning to her desk an hour later, Dr. Collins and his nephew returned to the office. Jackie had never seen the doctor so happy. He laughed and smiled and patted his nephew on the back. When he saw her, he grinned.

"Great news, Ms. Robbins. My nephew has decided to spend the next couple of weeks helping out in the office. Maybe we can convince him to stick around, eh?"

"Now, Uncle Bill, we discussed this." The nephew shot his uncle a look. "I'm just taking a break. I'm going back in a couple of weeks."

"We'll see about that." The doctor turned back to Jackie. "Make sure we set him up with an office and a few patients, okay?"

"Your nephew is a doctor, too?" Jackie was surprised.

"You bet. I taught him everything he knows."

"Well, not everything. I did go to medical school. Or at least that's what my student loan bills tell me."

Dr. Collins waved his hand. "Yes, but I taught you the important stuff: bedside manner and how to keep your patients." He winked at Jackie. "This guy's quite a charmer thanks to me."

The nephew laughed, and Jackie blushed. From his flirtatious smile, she had figured that out for herself. With a professional nod, her mind began to whir, getting the doctor's nephew set up. There was no shortage of patients to care for, but the office was a bit harder to come by. There was a little-used room at the end of the hallway that could be converted, but it would require work. And some furniture. But Jackie was nothing if not efficient, and she would take care of it.

It didn't take long for Paul to get settled. The cozy office his uncle's receptionist had arranged suited his purposes, and he found he enjoyed working with children. It was quite a change of pace from the whiny adults he usually dealt with. While he hadn't expected to work on his "vacation," he had quickly found himself growing bored. And boredom led his mind into uncomfortable territory. He had leapt at the opportunity to help out in his uncle's medical office. While he knew his uncle had ulterior motives – getting him to take over the practice, for one – he would take what he would get, one day at a time. With so much up in the air, it was all he could handle.

Paul had just sat down at his new desk when there was a tap on the door. He looked up to find the receptionist, Jackie, hovering in the doorway.

"Hi, Jackie. How can I help you?"

"I'm sorry to bother you, Dr. Casey, but Dr. Collins wanted me to make sure you were all set. Are you missing anything? Is your office all right?"

"My office is fine," he said, leaning back in his chair and smiling. "I thank you for getting it ready so quickly."

Jackie blushed. "It wasn't a problem. Your next appointment is at 3. Another flu, I'm afraid. I hope you don't get sick."

Paul laughed. "I've been around sick people for long enough. I think my immune system's the strongest it's ever been. I do feel bad for the kids, though. It can't be easy, especially with their parents hovering around them like they'll keel over if they sneeze."

Jackie gave him a small smile. "They can be rather overprotective, can't they?"

"Yes, they can. But I guess I can't blame them. They just want what's best for their precious babies. Just let me know when the appointment gets here."

"All right." Jackie closed the door softly.

Paul stared at the closed door with a pensive look. She was a tough one to figure out, that Jackie. Shy, quiet, reserved, and yet efficient and able to handle anything that was thrown her way. He wondered what her story was. With a shake of his head, he acknowledged he probably wouldn't be around long enough to find out. Besides, he had more important things to figure out – like how he was going to save his marriage.

Chapter 3

The house was quiet, as usual, when Jackie got home. Shuffling through the stack of mail, she closed the front door with her foot, then turned to lock it. A couple of bills, a catalog advertising holiday gifts, donation solicitations. Jackie sighed. Just once it would be nice to get a piece of mail that got her heart racing: a letter from a secret admirer, perhaps, or a gift from a stranger. Something exciting. Something other than bills and junk mail. But she supposed it was just her mind wishing she lived in a novel again.

Jackie's efficiency didn't stop at work, and she went through the motions of getting dinner ready. Once a month she prepared meals for herself, then divided them into individual servings and froze them in little containers. When it came time to eat, all she had to do was preheat the oven or toss the container in the microwave, and voilá . Dinner. Today's menu included lasagna, and Jackie decided to splurge by making some garlic bread to go with it. As the oven preheated, she sliced open a roll and prepared it, then slid it into her toaster oven.

While waiting for her dinner to be ready, Jackie sighed again. What was with her lately? Her life was routine, yes, but she was usually somewhat content. She didn't often get melancholy or restless. But ever since she had read the letter from Dr. Collins, it was as though everything she was unhappy with in her life was brought to the surface. It was as if she knew her life was going to be thrown into upheaval, and she wondered if she should just throw caution to the wind and change everything while she was at it.

Jackie's heart quickened. It was a terrifying thought, as most thoughts about change were for her. But perhaps she had already gotten a piece of mail that would make her heart start racing. Perhaps the letter from the doctor was her call to arms, her kick in the butt, to make her life more exciting, more challenging – more *interesting*. What would it be like? What would it feel like to just change everything all at once? Scary, yes. But she couldn't deny that part of her was excited at the thought. Maybe it wasn't just fear that was getting her heart pumping. Maybe it was the idea that she could really turn her life around.

The oven timer dinged, and Jackie jumped. As she went through the motions of serving and eating her meal, her mind continued to whir. Tomorrow was book club, and she was going to talk to Mary. A lot had changed in Mary's life – as evidenced by the wedding ring and growing belly – and Jackie could use a little advice. This time, though, she would actually do something about it. This time she wouldn't just talk about making changes. She would actually *make* some changes.

Jackie's heart started racing again. It was scary. But she was 35 years old. If she didn't make changes now, when would she? Would she be alone, stuck in the same routine, for the rest of her life? The thought was depressing, and it gave her just enough added motivation to make her mind up. It was time to make some changes. And this time, *she* would be the one deciding what would change.

Jackie was the first one at book club, as usual. She hoped Mary would be on time. Mary usually came straight from school to browse the library stacks, so she tended to be early, too. As Jackie waited, she couldn't keep her foot from tapping. She had been so fidgety lately. She was usually the calm, quiet one. Now she could barely keep still. And part of her wanted to yell "fire!" in a crowded room. The thought made her giggle.

Mary entered the room after a few minutes, and, with a smile at Jackie, proceeded to the refreshment table to get a couple of cookies before sitting at the empty chair beside Jackie.

"Hey, Jackie, how's it going?"

Jackie nearly breathed a sigh of relief. At last, someone she could talk to. "Different."

Mary looked up at her with arched eyebrows. "Different?"

Jackie closed her eyes. "Remember how I said last year that I wanted to make some changes in my life?"

"Of course. But you never told me how that went."

"It didn't. I was too scared to change much."

"I can understand that. You get comfortable with a certain way of life, even if you're not quite happy."

"Exactly. But now I'm not comfortable."

"Did something happen?"

"Kind of." Jackie enlightened Mary about the letter from her boss, and the frightening, heart-pounding revelations she had come to the previous evening.

Mary laughed.

It wasn't the response Jackie had been expecting, and she didn't know how to react.

Mary rested a hand on Jackie's arm. "Please don't think I'm laughing at you. I just understand all-too-well how scary and yet exhilarating it can be to decide to make changes in your life. And if the deer-in-headlights look in your eyes is any indication, you don't even know where to start. I've been there."

Jackie eased back in her chair. "So what do I do?"

"Well, you have to decide what you want. What do you want to be? To do? Do you want to change careers? Do you want to find someone and be in a relationship? Do you want to take up new hobbies? Do you want to move somewhere new?"

Jackie sighed. "I have no idea."

"Then that's where I would start. For me, I was lonely. I wanted to be in a relationship with a man who respected me for me, and I wanted to start a family." Mary rested a hand on her slightly-round belly. "I've been successful, but a lot of that was luck, too. And fate. Timing. Whatever you want to call it. But I had to put myself out there, acknowledge what I wanted and who I wanted to be. I never would have met Bryan if I hadn't decided to go out and meet people, go dancing and take a chance. Sometimes you have to take a leap of faith."

Paul lay on the bed in his uncle's guest room, arms tucked behind his head, staring at the ceiling. He had been struggling with insomnia since he had arrived, but it hadn't started bothering him too much yet. It was a great opportunity to think, to process his uncle's advice without Bill trying to convince him to move nearby and take over the medical practice. The gentle sounds of nature at night soothed his senses and helped him admit, if only to himself, how he really felt about everything.

His marriage had been disintegrating for a while now. He could acknowledge that. But they had been married ten years. Every relationship had its weak points, didn't it? He figured they could work through their problems and push through. Heck, he had even agreed to see a couples' therapist. That had to count for something, didn't it?

But Pam had said it was too late. She wasn't in love with him anymore. She didn't want to try and save their marriage. She cared about him, yes, but it wasn't enough. Not anymore. That was when she said she wanted a divorce. He had been struck dumb. But he lived in denial for a couple of weeks, until Pam had issued her ultimatum. Get out or be thrown out. Not much of a choice. What could he do?

The question now was: did he want to fight for her? They shared a past, and he did love her. But what she had said, about not being in love with him – it really struck a chord. Was that how he felt, too? Was he holding on to a shell of a marriage because of a mutual history? Because of a feeling of obligation? Did he love Pam, but had fallen out of love with her?

Paul rubbed a hand down his face. He was exhausted. It had been a long day, filled with patients. He was grateful for the distraction, for the activity to keep him occupied, but he couldn't live in denial forever. He had to make some decisions. He had been with his uncle almost a week already. That meant only one more week to figure out if he was going home to fight, or if he was walking away. It wasn't an easy decision, especially when he couldn't even describe how he was feeling. Pam deserved to be happy. He did, too. Would walking away from their marriage make them happy? Or would fixing what had gone wrong make them happy? Could it be fixed? Was it worth fixing?

What a mess. Then, of course, there was his uncle to consider. He had asked for advice, and Uncle Bill had been more than accommodating. But the subtle, or not-so-subtle, pressure to take over the practice had been more effective than Paul cared to admit. The idea held appeal. What would it be like to own his own practice, to answer to only himself? And the kids – the kids were great. He had never been interested in pediatrics, but the more time he spent with the kids, the more he found he enjoyed it.

He and Pam had never had a desire to start their own family, and he had never felt like he was missing out. He just figured he wasn't a kid person. Some were cut out to be parents; he and Pam weren't. But spending time with his new patients tugged a bit on his heartstrings. He wondered if he would have been so bad at it. Of course, he wasn't getting any younger, nor was Pam. And Pam had always been more interested in her career than in being a mother. But even if they got back together, and decided to start a family, it would be a lot harder now. They were both pushing 40. Not impossible, but less likely. But if he took over the practice, he would get to know these kids, care for these kids and fill that little hole in his heart that he hadn't known existed until recently.

But if he and Pam got back together, the commute would be too much. An hour each way was doable, but it held no appeal, especially after a long, busy day. Which meant something would have to give.

Paul rolled onto his side. It was no wonder he had insomnia, with all this running through his head. There were too many decisions to make, and not enough time to make them in. How could he decide the entire course of his life in one week? Did he just have to jump in and hope he would swim? That he wouldn't fall apart and drown? But where would he jump? When? How? With a sigh Paul closed his eyes and decided to count sheep instead.

Chapter 4

The office was surprisingly quiet Thursday morning. The phones were still, the waiting room nearly empty. Usually on mornings like this Jackie would take out a book and quietly read at the desk, waiting for the bell above the front door to jingle. Or she would catch up on office tasks: fill up the copier, make sure there weren't any supplies that needed ordering. Or she would take care of the filing that began to accumulate once in a while.

But the tasks were done, and she was too restless to read. She found herself staring out the window at one side of the waiting room, watching the puffy clouds roll by. It was a beautiful fall day. It made her want to go out and pick apples or something. Maybe carve a pumpkin.

With a sigh Jackie looked down at the pad of paper by her hand. She had spent the past five minutes tapping a pencil on the desk, trying to get her brain to cooperate. She had been trying to do what Mary had suggested: figure out what it was she wanted. What did she want to change? What about her life made her unhappy? But she wasn't getting anywhere. It was almost as if she didn't want to admit how unhappy she was. She didn't want to acknowledge that she had made some bad choices, or been a coward, or taken the path of least resistance. Would changing who she was take away all that she had been?

With a deep breath for courage, Jackie put pencil to paper. What could she start with that wouldn't be too scary? Okay. Get more hobbies. She wrote that down. She had way too much free time, and while she enjoyed reading, she really needed something more worthwhile to do, too. Maybe she would get back into volunteering. She wrote that down, too.

Jackie sat, deep in thought, until a noise startled her out of her reverie. She turned to find Dr. Casey standing by her right shoulder.

"Whatcha doing?" He glanced at the paper in front of Jackie. Almost protectively, Jackie slid her hand over the elegant lettering.

"Nothing." She blushed.

Dr. Casey grinned. "Doesn't look like nothing. It looked like you were making a list."

"I'm sorry. I'll get back to work." Jackie scrambled to her feet, flipping over the notepad in the process.

Dr. Casey put a hand on her shoulder. "Relax. I was just making conversation. It's not as if it's hopping in here. You're allowed to take a breather. Have a seat."

Jackie fell back into the chair. Dr. Casey propped himself on the counter a couple of feet away.

"How long have you been working here, Jackie?"

"Um. It'll be ten years in November."

"Wow. You like it here?"

Jackie nodded. "I do. I love working with the kids, and Dr. Collins is a great boss."

"I'm glad to hear it."

"What kind of work do you usually do?"

"I work in a pretty big office. I studied internal medicine, but the office handles all kinds of cases. General PCP-type stuff."

"Do you like it?"

Dr. Casey shrugged. "It's all right. Some of the patients crack me up. They come in for every little thing. And then you get the patients who have something seriously wrong with them, and they avoid the doctor like the plague."

"Sometimes it's easier to live in denial than to do something about it."

"You sound as if you're speaking from experience."

It was Jackie's turn to shrug. "It's easy to get complacent. And even if you suspect there may be something wrong, it can be hard to face that fact."

Dr. Casey looked down and scraped a toe at the carpet. "I know that feeling all too well."

Jackie looked down to where Dr. Casey's foot was making circles on the carpet. She wasn't one to pry, but she suspected Dr. Casey had some things on his mind, too. But how could she ask?

He looked up and smiled, and the moment passed. "So what do you do in your spare time, Jackie?'

Jackie took a deep breath and attempted a smile. "Read mostly. Not much else."

"Are you married?"

"No."

"I'm sorry. I probably shouldn't have asked that."

"It's okay. Are you married?"

Dr. Casey nodded. "Yeah. But we're separated at the moment. That's why I'm hanging out with Uncle Bill." He grinned again, but the smile didn't quite reach his eyes.

"I'm sorry."

"It is what it is, I guess. She wants out. But enough about my problems. There's no reason for us to get depressed at work. Especially when I'm supposed to be on vacation."

"Some vacation." Jackie risked a grin. He grinned back.

"Tell me about it."

They sat in companionable silence for a moment. Jackie looked at the up-side-down notepad and sighed.

"So what kind of list were you making? Grocery list?"

He seemed overly curious, but maybe he was just trying to make conversation. Maybe it would be nice to talk to someone else about it. With a sigh she flipped the paper back over. "I've decided to make some changes in my life. A friend suggested I start by figuring out what it is I want to change. So I've been trying to make a list of things I want to change."

"Huh. So what have you got so far?"

Jackie looked up and met his eyes. The questions were borderline rude, but he seemed sincere. Maybe he was looking for a distraction from his own problems. "Not much. I'm not a big fan of change."

"Then why the decision to make changes?"

"I guess I'm just tired of living in denial." She sighed again. "And Dr. Collins is retiring, so it's not as if I have a say in the matter when it comes to certain things. I figured I might as well do it all at once. Rip the band-aid off fast to save pain in the long run."

"Interesting analogy. Are you expecting it to be a painful experience?"

Jackie shrugged. "Most of the changes I've experienced have been out of my control. Just when I thought I was settled, someone does something that throws my life into upheaval."

"Like Bill retiring."

"Exactly. So the experiences haven't been all that pleasant, because they've been unexpected and disconcerting. I could use some positive change, but I honestly don't know what to expect from this decision."

"I find myself in a similar situation, strange as it may seem."

"Because of your wife?"

Dr. Casey gave her a sad smile. "Yeah. I have some decisions to make, and no matter what I decide, things are going to have to change. The process hasn't been very pleasant, but I'm hoping the outcome will be."

"Exactly."

Dr. Casey stood up. "This conversation has been most enlightening. You've definitely given me a lot to think about."

"Glad I could be of service?"

Dr. Casey grinned. "Maybe we can help each other. We're both trying to figure out what we want. Maybe we can be our own support group. That is, if you don't mind?"

Jackie thought for a moment. It would be nice to have a sounding board. But she barely knew Dr. Casey. Did that make it easier or harder? "I don't mind."

"Great! Then I'll let you get back to your list. I may have a list of my own to make. Maybe we can trade notes later."

"Sure."

He left the office then, and Jackie watched his retreating back. He was a strange man, she decided. Nice, but strange.

Paul collapsed into the chair behind his desk, then put his head in his hands. What was wrong with him? What was he doing, interrogating the poor receptionist? That had been rude, plain and simple. But curiosity had gotten the better of him. He wanted to know more about her, about what made her tick. And he couldn't make himself regret it. Who would have thought they would be in the same boat? Stuck making changes they didn't know if they were ready to make. Scared to take that giant leap, but scared what would happen if they didn't. Not even sure what that leap really entailed.

He may have bullied her into it, but it would be nice to have someone other than Uncle Bill to talk about this with. Maybe she could give him the woman's perspective on everything, help him see what Pam was feeling. Then again, maybe he was putting too much stock into a simple encounter. Maybe Jackie would want nothing to do with him.

Paul sighed and leaned back in his chair. Then he took out a pad of paper and a pencil. Maybe it was time to make a list of his own. With determination he wrote at the top of the paper "What I Want." Simple, straightforward. Scribbled in his less-than-neat handwriting, it looked frantic, hurried. Like he was anxious to get this over with. How true that was.

Okay. Number one. *To be happy.* Then he erased it. That was too broad, too general. He needed something more tangible. He spent a moment tapping the pencil on the notepad. And tapping some more. Then he threw down the pencil in frustration. He had no idea what he wanted. That was the problem. How was he supposed to figure out what to do if he didn't even know what he wanted?

Paul leaned back in his chair and closed his eyes. His thoughts wandered, as they usually did when he was lying in bed awake at night. He hadn't come to any conclusions about Pam, about taking over the office, about anything, really. And it still all boiled down to that one question: what would make him happy? Maybe he should just do what Jackie was doing: throw caution to the wind and change everything all at once. But it wasn't that simple. How could he so nonchalantly throw away ten years of marriage? He didn't think it was possible, and yet Pam seemed willing to do it. And would that make him happy, or would he be as miserable as he was now?

Maybe what he really needed was to take a break from all this over-analyzing. Maybe he needed to spend the remaining week of his "vacation" not thinking about Pam, or their situation, or what to do with his life. Maybe he needed to figure out what he really wanted.

Paul ripped off the top sheet of paper and started a new list: what he would like to experience. Places to go, activities to try, people to meet. There was so much he had always wanted to do, and he had never had the opportunity. Either he was in school, struggling to make good grades, or he was married, and Pam had no desire to do the things he wanted to. Actually, there were a lot of things he wanted to do that Pam had discouraged him from. Some he could understand, like skydiving. But taking a cross-country road trip? What was so bad about that? Paul's fingers could barely keep up with the ideas that were flowing freely now. Everything he had ever considered doing, scribbled down on a pad of paper.

Soon he had filled three sheets, and he was exhausted. He was startled to see that nearly an hour had passed. And on his desk, in black and white, were all the disappointments of the past fifteen years. It had turned into more than a list of the big things he hoped to accomplish. It had somehow become a list of little things that Pam had shot down: buying a red car instead of a blue car ("red cars cost more to insure"), shaving his beard ("a beard makes you look more distinguished as a doctor"), even working at an established practice instead of breaking out on his own ("how are we going to pay our bills if you don't get patients?"). He found himself wanting to do all those things just to spite Pam. Why had he let her control his life for so long? Because he loved her? If *she* had loved *him*, wouldn't she have wanted him to be happy?

He was going to shave his beard that night. Just because he wanted to. Because he could. And when his lease was up, he was trading it in for a red car. A red *sports* car. That would show her. And it would serve her right if he took over the practice here. An hour commute? He could always get an apartment nearby. They could do the separate thing during the week and then spend weekends together. Would that work?

With a sigh he had to acknowledge that "getting back" at Pam wouldn't solve anything. He had to do things because he wanted to, not because he wanted to teach her a lesson. But he had spent so long listening to the Pam in his head that it was a hard habit to break. What did he *really* want? Did he want what he thought he wanted because it was what Pam wanted? Or what Pam *didn't* want? Or did he actually really want it?

Paul rubbed a hand over his face in frustration. This was getting to be even harder than he thought. But maybe he had to start small, ease himself into things. Maybe he really would shave his beard tonight. He could see how he felt afterward. He had grown used to his beard, and even if the reason for keeping it had been Pam, maybe changing things up would let him know if he was ready for bigger changes. He was almost excited to see what he would look like. For twelve years he had had that beard. Decision made, he leaned back in his chair again. A little change. It was a start. And he felt good about at least deciding that.

Chapter 5

Jackie didn't recognize the man who had just walked into the office, but he greeted her with a smile and attempted to walk into the office.

"Excuse me, can I help you?"

The man laughed. "I know. It's a big change, right? I hardly recognize myself!"

Jackie's jaw dropped open. "Dr. Casey? Is that you?"

Dr. Casey rubbed his jaw and smiled. "Yup. What do you think?"

"I don't even know what to think! It's definitely different."

The smile faded. "Bad different? Is it too much?"

"No, no, not bad different. It'll just take some getting used to."

"Hmm. Do I look less distinguished?"

Jackie cocked her head to one side and analyzed the man in front of her. He was definitely an attractive man. More so now, at least in Jackie's opinion. But she had never been a fan of facial hair to begin with. She cleared her throat. "You look younger, but I don't think that's a bad thing. You have kind eyes, and I think that speaks more for you than a beard would, especially with kids."

"So you don't think I look less respectable as a doctor without a beard?"

"I wouldn't say so, no. Plenty of doctors don't have beards."

Dr. Casey patted her shoulder. "Thanks, Jackie. I think I needed to hear that."

He left the front office then and headed to his room in the back, leaving Jackie curious. She guessed his decision to shave had been part of the changes they had both discussed. It was nice to know at least one of them had been brave enough to do something, even if it was a small action like that. With the weekend looming, and her "support group" moving forward without her, Jackie's resolve built. She would make changes this weekend, too. She just didn't know what yet.

Jackie's response had been encouraging. He hadn't known what kind of reaction to expect, but it was nice to know he didn't lose any credibility simply because he no longer had facial hair. Paul rubbed his jaw line again. He liked it. Though it would have been a more beneficial experience in the summer, when it was hot, than the fall, when it was getting cooler, he found he liked the freeing sensation. His face was lighter. No more itching. And Jackie was right: he did look younger. Before, looking older had made him *feel* older. Partnered with the life decisions he had to make, the feeling had left him rundown. Maybe this lighter, more youthful vibe would extend to the rest of his life, too. He could hope.

Paul settled into his chair and pulled out the notepad he had started his list of goals on. With a smile and a flourish, he checked off shaving his beard. It may be a small change, but it was something. What should be next? He would have to give it some thought.

During a lull that afternoon, Jackie knocked tentatively on his door. He beckoned her in and put down the chart he was examining.

"Hey, Jackie. How's it going?"

She seemed taken aback by his casual attitude. Maybe he was taking his youthful feeling a little too far. "It's going okay."

"What can I do for you?"

"Um."

Paul waited in silence for a moment for Jackie to continue. "Jackie?"

She looked up at him, distracted. "Hmm?"

"Did you need something?"

"Oh. Yeah." She looked down shyly, moving one foot against the other. Then she took a deep breath and looked back up, meeting his eyes. "How did you do it?"

"Do what?"

"Get the motivation to actually change something? Every time I think of something to change, I stop. I get almost paralyzed with fear."

"Well, that's kind of why I started with something easy. I figured if I didn't like it, it would grow back. Maybe you should start with something easy that doesn't have too many repercussions if you don't like it."

"I've thought of that. But I still can't seem to get myself to do anything about it."

"Well, maybe I can help."

"Okay."

"What is it that you've thought about changing? Start with the easy stuff."

"Hmm. Well, I've thought about getting more hobbies."

"That's an easy one. What would you like to do?"

"I don't know. That's the problem. It sounds easy, but the execution is much more difficult."

"I found, when making my lists, that it was more productive to write down concrete things I wanted to do, rather than abstract concepts. So instead of saying "get more hobbies," try writing down hobbies you've thought about trying in the past. You don't actually have to do any of them if they no longer appeal to you. But if it's something you've thought about doing before, maybe you'll come up with something you want to do now."

"Okay. I'll try that. Thanks."

"No problem."

Jackie left the office then, quietly closing the door behind her. Paul's eyes stayed on the closed door for a moment as he processed what had just happened. He found it amazing that someone who was so good at her job, so efficient and responsible, would be so timid when it came to her own life. It was like work was her comfort zone, and real life was awkward.

With a half laugh, Paul acknowledged that it was probably the same for a lot of people, himself included. Why else would he have opted to work on his time away? It was easier to forget his problems when he was focused on a patient's concerns. At work he knew where he stood. There were only so many courses of action, and education and experience usually led him to the ones that would be the most beneficial. When it came to his current life situation, it wasn't so simple.

He didn't have similar experiences. There was no one to tell him what the best course of action would be. All anyone could give him was advice, and that advice was usually based on unrelated experience -- or no experience at all. It was no wonder he found himself floundering. Work and life were in completely different realms, and he found he much preferred the comforting familiarity of medicine.

What he needed to do, he decided, was break out of his comfort zone, make it so work wasn't an option. At least until he came to some kind of conclusion about what to do. But his vacation time was almost up. If he didn't return to work -- his real job -- next week, there was a chance he wouldn't have a job to go back to. And that made him nervous. He loved his job. Then again...

Paul looked down at the file he had been reviewing before Jackie walked in. It was a thick file, filled with tests and doctor visits and prescriptions. The poor child -- at the ripe age of five -- had been through more than many of his elderly patients. It broke his heart, and yet these were the cases he was drawn to most. If he could help this child, he could make a dramatic difference in not only his life, but the lives of his parents, relatives and friends. Wasn't that why he had gotten into medicine in the first place? To make a difference? The patients he saw now weren't bad. And, yes, he had made a difference in many of their lives. Sent them for tests when something was wrong, prescribed them medications to treat what ailed them. They were grateful. But maybe it was time for a change. Maybe the kids he had met here needed him more than the adults he had been working with. Would he be happy taking over his uncle's practice?

Paul's heart started racing. It would be a big adjustment, but an exciting one. But he had to acknowledge the risks. The commute, for one, would greatly affect his chances of getting back together with Pam. Was he okay with that? And being in business for himself was a big risk -- made bigger by the fact that Pam had never wanted him to take that risk. Would that affect his chances with her, too?

Paul ran a hand down his face. He needed time to think -- really think -- and he wasn't going to get it sitting in an office with patients lining up to see him. He needed to get away for a little bit, get some perspective. He would finish out the day here, and then take the rest of the week off. Maybe then he could figure out what he wanted to do.

Jackie was grateful for a quiet office. Even the occasional patient didn't affect her ability to think about her situation. She could do most of her job by rote, so her brain could continue to process and ponder as she worked. Perhaps that was one of the reasons she liked her job so much: she knew what to expect and what to do. She didn't have to worry about doing things properly, because she just did them.

But the one thing she was sure about might get taken away from her. She had to keep reminding herself of that. All this change she was proposing was not just for the heck of it. There was a reason for it. And the better she prepared herself, maybe the easier this big change would be.

So. Starting with something easy. Hobbies. What did she want to do? She thought back to what Dr. Casey had suggested. She had had lots of ideas throughout her life: knitting, horseback riding, writing. She loved to cook, and had considered taking classes to learn about different kinds of cuisine. But who would she cook for? She lived alone. She supposed she could invite some people over, maybe the members of her book club. But the thought of entertaining made her nervous. She wasn't very sociable -- and that was as a guest. As a hostess, she would need to make sure everyone's needs were met, that the conversation didn't lag, that people were having a good time. Dinner parties were a lot of pressure. And that was assuming the food was delicious. If she was nervous about the rest of the party, there was a decent chance she'd mess up on the food, too. And it wouldn't help her on her quest to be a failure at her first attempt. Still, there was something that drew her in. She would have to give it some thought.

She supposed it wouldn't hurt to take a class, perhaps one of the continuing education classes that the high school offered. A few sessions might give her just the taste she was looking for. No reason to go into a panic over dinner parties unnecessarily. She took a deep breath and wrote "take a cooking class" on her new list.

Actually, taking classes might not be a bad idea -- and not just for cooking, either. She was interested in meeting new people -- especially of the male variety, she thought with a blush -- and classes would give her the opportunity to try out new hobbies and meet new people at the same time. For the first time since starting this project, Jackie smiled. At last, she had something concrete she could do. She was going to swing by the high school after work and pick up a course book. Who knew what else they might offer that would interest her? The possibilities were truly endless, and for once thinking about the options was getting her excited, instead of filling her with dread.

Chapter 6

Uncle Bill was accommodating when Paul told him he wanted to stop going to the office. Paul didn't know what he would do with all his free time, but he knew he needed to step back from work to get a real feel for what he wanted to do.

The weekend with Uncle Bill flew by, but three hours into his first day alone he was already going stark raving mad. This had been the problem when he first arrived. Why did he have such a hard time in his own company? Was it that he just didn't want to think about the decisions that had to be made? Or was he really that miserable outside of work? He had never noticed it before. But before, Pam had always planned out nearly every spare minute. There wasn't time to think. There wasn't time to figure out what he wanted to do, how he wanted to spend his time.

The more he thought about it, the more it seemed to him that Pam had really controlled all aspects of his life. It was as if he didn't know who to be without her. It was a scary thought. Could a list of what he used to want to do be all that remained of his individual self? Had the rest of him disappeared into the oblivion that was his marriage?

Paul meandered onto his uncle's back deck. He had always liked his uncle's house. It was comfortable, warm, and it had a great view. The backyard was filled with trees, and the house was situated on a slight hill, giving it a vantage point to overlook the mountains in the distance. It was rustic and charming, without being reminiscent of a hunting lodge or campsite. In Paul's mind, it was perfect. And looking out over nature gave him something to think about other than his pathetic existence.

It was sad to think of his uncle living here alone. He was sure Uncle Bill missed Aunt Sarah, though he never talked about her. But living in this house, filled with memories of their life together, must be difficult. He couldn't imagine living in his house without Pam. The house symbolized their life, their marriage, their hopes and dreams for the future. It would seem huge and empty without her. It would be a symbol of their failure instead of their love. It was a depressing thought.

With a sigh Paul collapsed into one of the Adirondack chairs on the deck. A moment later he found himself playing with the ring on his left hand. He was tempted to yank it off and throw it into the trees. But he found he wasn't quite ready to surrender all hope. Maybe he should fight for Pam. His life was apparently completely intertwined with hers. It had to be easier than trying to tear himself apart and figure out who he was. But was easier better? Probably not. So did that mean it was better to walk away? He had started out thinking that walking away would be easier, which meant it would be the worse choice. But now -- now he saw that it would be much, much harder. Maybe it would make him a stronger person. Maybe he would be happier if he reconnected with who he used to be. Or maybe it would reinforce how miserable he was without Pam.

He couldn't win. Either way it looked like he would be miserable. And what if he fought for Pam and lost? Then he would be miserable and a failure. That could be more than he could bear. No one liked being a failure.

Change was scary. He could definitely agree with Jackie on that one. No matter what happened, there would be major changes taking place. And he wasn't sure he liked any of his options. The more he thought about it, the more he wanted to just crawl under a rock and pretend everything was okay. But, obviously, that was not an option.

Paul rubbed his chin with one hand and grinned. The one change he had made still agreed with him. He had shaved again this morning, and he was liking the freedom of a clean jaw. Maybe it was all about baby steps. Maybe, like he had recommended to Jackie, it was about making the little changes before you had to jump into the big ones. So what other changes could he make? What else could he cross off his list that would help him feel a little closer to his goals -- and his decisions?

The paper was crumpled by now, heavy creases marking the once-clean sheets. He had looked at them so often it was amazing they hadn't ripped by now -- and that he hadn't memorized their contents.

Some of the items on the list had long since lost their appeal. Skydiving, for one, no longer sounded exciting. And heading to Times Square for New Year's Eve sounded needlessly reckless. He was bound to get trampled. These were great ideas for a twenty-something college kid, but for a grown man pushing forty, his priorities had changed. His eyes scanned the list, looking for something, anything, that sparked his interest. Every time he did this, his eyes were drawn to the same two items -- the same items that Pam had turned him away from time and time again -- taking a cross-country road trip and starting his own practice.

Neither was a small change. Neither would be easy, or cheap. And if he wanted to get back together with Pam, neither was a feasible option. The road trip wouldn't really affect the long term in and of itself, but the time spent on such an excursion could mean a lost opportunity to save his marriage, not to mention his job. Was he willing to take that risk on something so frivolous? And, of course, the cons of taking over his uncle's practice had been turned over so many times in his brain that he was tired of thinking about them. And yet...

He had always heard that everything happens for a reason. Was there a reason he had turned to Uncle Bill in his time of need? And that his time of need happened to coincide with Bill's desire to retire? Was there a reason he had met Jackie and connected with her over their mutual need to change their lives? And if everything happened for a reason, then maybe even if he decided to take those massive leaps, what ended up happening would be what was destined to happen. If he was supposed to get back together with Pam, maybe being apart for a couple more weeks would make her miss him more, realize what she was giving up. Maybe him taking over his uncle's practice would show her that he was stronger than she seemed to think he was, that he was capable of standing on his own two feet.

Was he really trying to change just to show Pam how wrong she was?

Paul closed his eyes and leaned back in the chair. It seemed the more he thought about things, the more confused he got. He still had no idea what to do, and it was really starting to frustrate him. Part of him was tired, fed up with the way that Pam seemed to have a say in everything he said and did. But part of him still loved her, wanted to fight for her, refuse to divorce her, anything to save their marriage. It wasn't an easy decision. But was it even his decision to make? If Pam really wanted a divorce that badly, could he really refuse? The decision may be completely out of his control, and here he was driving himself nuts about it.

Maybe he should call Pam.

The idea popped into his head quickly and unexpectedly, and he immediately knew he had to act. He couldn't possibly make this decision on his own. There were two people involved here, two people whose lives would undoubtedly change with whatever decision took place. He couldn't decide his course of action while sitting an hour away in a thought bubble of his own. He needed to discuss it with the one other person who would understand what was going on and what would be given up.

He pushed himself off the chair and pulled his phone out of his pocket, then he paused. Would she answer the phone if she knew it was him? He went inside and grabbed his uncle's cordless phone instead. He dialed the number by memory and waited for it to ring.

She sounded breathless when she answered the phone, as if she had just run inside. "Hello?"

"Hi, Pam."

"Paul." She sounded surprised to hear from him, and silence fell for a moment. "I didn't expect it to be you."

"Who did you expect it to be?"

"Pretty much anybody else."

"Sorry."

"It's okay. What's up?"

Now that he had her on the phone, he had no idea what to say. What could he tell her that would make sense of the mess that had been flowing through his head? That he missed her but didn't know if he should fight for her or not, that he was starting to rethink certain aspects of his career, that he wanted to just run away from it all for a while and see the world instead of the same four walls day in and day out? "I just wanted to see how you were doing."

"I'm fine. How are you?"

"Confused."

Pam sighed but didn't say anything.

"I don't know what to do, Pam."

"About what? The papers should reach you in a couple of days. Just sign them and send them back."

"Is that what you really want?"

"I told you it was."

"I just thought..."

"Thought what, Paul?" She was frustrated now, impatient with him.

"I thought that you might miss me as much as I missed you."

"I do miss you."

Paul's heart lifted a bit.

"But that doesn't change anything."

His heart fell. "Why not?"

"Because I knew I would miss you. That wasn't in question. But just because you get used to having someone around doesn't mean you should stay with him."

"I didn't think that was the only reason we were still together."

"I wasn't happy, Paul. How many times did I tell you? It's not as if I just woke up one morning and decided I wanted a divorce. It was a long time coming."

"You might have let me in on it."

"I told you! So many times, that I was unhappy."

"I thought you meant at the moment, with your job or something."

"If I'm unhappy in the moment every day, what does that tell you?"

Paul pulled out a dining chair and fell into it. This conversation was not going the way he had expected. "We could still fix this. We could still go to therapy."

Pam sighed again. "It's too late, Paul. I'm not in love with you anymore. There's no reason for me to fight for this."

"Don't I get a say?"

"Don't act like the victim here, Paul. You had as much of a part in this as I did. And if you didn't do anything about it in the past, I don't think anything you do now will help. It's too little, too late. I'm sorry."

If it was any consolation, she did sound contrite. But was that really it? Was there nothing he could do?

"I still love you, Pam."

"I love you too, Paul. A part of me always will. But I'm not *in* love with you. The love I have for you is linked to the fond memories and a shared history. It has nothing to do with any kind of romantic attachment in the present. And I'm sorry, but it's not enough. I can't live a stagnant life because I'm trying to hold on to the past."

"So that's it? Ten years down the drain?"

"See? You're doing it, too. You're thinking more about the past than the present. Were you happy, Paul? Looking back at the past year or so, were you really happy?"

The question caught Paul off guard, though he had found himself thinking very similar thoughts himself over the past week and a half. He found he still had no answer.

"I have to go, Paul."

"Okay."

"I'm sorry you're so upset. But I really think this is best. And not just for me." She paused a moment. "Take care."

There was a soft click as she hung up the phone, then an incessant beeping while Paul still held the phone in his hand.

Well, the conversation had solved one problem: he had one less decision to make. His marriage was over.

Jackie was surprised to see Dr. Casey walk into the office Wednesday afternoon. She was under the impression that he wasn't coming back, that he was off to his old life. But she guessed he wasn't there to work. He was dressed in jeans and a t-shirt and walked with purpose toward the back office. A moment later she heard the door to Dr. Collins's office click shut.

Jackie respected their privacy, but she couldn't help but be curious. Dr. Casey had looked determined, anxious, and he had greeted her with nothing more than a nod. It was a far cry from the jovial, upbeat man she had seen only a day earlier.

The meeting was brief, perhaps due to the line of patients that was waiting to get seen, and the man that walked out of the office was more relaxed, relieved, than the one who had walked in. He entered the front office where Jackie sat and propped himself on the side counter.

"So, Jackie, it looks like I'll be seeing a lot more of you after all."

Jackie lifted her eyebrows but said nothing.

"I'm taking over Uncle Bill's practice."

Her initial reaction was shock, followed by an immense sense of relief. Her career wasn't over. She didn't have to go anywhere. Maybe she didn't even have to make any changes...

"I won't be starting until next month, though. Uncle Bill will continue as scheduled. He'll be sending out letters to his patients and such. I imagine he'll have you write them up."

Thoughts raced through Jackie's brain, and she grasped the first one that made sense. "What will you be doing until then?"

He grinned, and more of the man she had met returned. "I'll be quitting my current job, of course. And then I'll be doing something I've always wanted to do: taking a road trip."

"A road trip?"

"Yup. My thought was a cross-country trip, but I may start with just the east coast to get my feet wet. I haven't decided yet."

"Wow."

"Yeah. The timing is perfect. I don't know when I'll get another opportunity to do this."

Jackie's mind was still attempting to process this latest bit of information when he dropped a bombshell.

"I'd like you to come with me."

Brain occupied, it took Jackie a minute to really comprehend what he was saying. "Excuse me?"

"I think you should join me on my road trip. I think it'll do us both good to get away from real life for a bit, see the sites, think about life. Maybe it'll help get us both back on track."

A road trip? With Dr. Casey? She barely knew the man! What could he possibly be thinking?

"I'm sure you want to think about it."

Jackie could only nod.

"I'm heading back home for a few days to tie up the loose ends there. Think it over while I'm gone. I'll be back at the end of next week."

Jackie nodded again. "Okay." It was all she could acknowledge.

Dr. Casey grinned again, then blew out of the office, leaving Jacking speechless.

Chapter 7

Returning home was bittersweet for Paul. It was strange being in town and knowing he couldn't go to the house he had spent the last ten years living in. He wondered what they would do with it once the divorce was final. It was a great house, but with his taking over his uncle's practice, it wouldn't make sense for him to live there anymore. Maybe he would just let Pam have it. But what would he get? He hated the thought of dividing up all of their possessions, but he supposed there was no other option, unless he just walked away with nothing. And that didn't make much sense. He would have to establish a life of his own now, and he would need things to get started. Not to mention he had paid for most of those things before Pam's career had gotten off the ground.

But it didn't matter. Not really. He was just distracting himself from the pain that had hit his gut as soon as he approached the exit. He guessed he'd have to stay in a hotel for the week. He didn't want to be a burden on any of his friends and their families, and it made no sense to look for somewhere permanent since he would be moving. So the generic room of a hotel chain would have to suffice.

What he hadn't decided was if he would work the week at his old job or just hand in his letter of resignation and leave. There wasn't anything holding him there, other than a sense of obligation, but what else would he do for the week?

He probably should have just said he'd be back at his uncle's on Monday. But he wanted to give Jackie time to think about what he had proposed. He knew he had shocked her. And he had no idea if she would accept or not. But he really wanted to take the road trip, and the thought of going alone was less appealing. He liked Jackie. But more than that, he thought it would help her, too. He knew she didn't like change, and maybe just being thrown into the deep end would help her learn how to swim.

He hoped he wasn't making a mistake. The last conversation with Pam had thrown him for a loop, and he had just taken it as a sign to do what he had been toying with anyway. But had he really thought it through? Maybe he had just been so grateful to have one less decision to make that he had just gone with whatever would be the quickest end to his mental torture.

Yet something about it felt right. He had enjoyed working with his young patients over the past week. The practice was established, the employees competent and efficient. As long as too many patients didn't pull out, he should be fine. The biggest adjustment would really be his life outside of the office. There would be no hiding then. He couldn't rely on Pam to plan out his days or provide a distraction when he was tired of his own company. Was that why he wanted Jackie to come with him? So he wouldn't be left alone with his own thoughts?

Paul pulled into the parking lot of the local Holiday Inn and turned off the engine. He needed to get a life. He needed something else to think about. Maybe he would start planning out his road trip. Whether or not Jackie wanted to go with him, he would still be making the journey. Did it make more sense to start up north at Maine, or down south at Florida? Either way the starting and ending trips would be long, though they could always stop and see the sites along the way, even if they would be deviating from the east coast.

It was good to get his mind on more positive things. He needed to look to the future, not dwell on the past. What happened with Pam was somewhat out of his hands. The papers would be waiting for him when he returned to Uncle Bill's, and that would be that. He would get a lawyer and show up in court when he was told to. He wouldn't say it would be easy, but dwelling on it served no purpose. His road trip, his plans for the future -- those were things he could control. The rest Pam had made abundantly clear was non-negotiable.

One week. That was all the time Jackie had to come up with an answer for Dr. Casey. Her initial reaction was just to say "no." There was no way she could take time off from work to go gallivanting with a man she barely knew -- a married man, at that -- and "find herself." It was ridiculous.

But the more she thought about it, the more she found herself coming up with reasons why it wasn't a bad idea. She had plenty of vacation time built up that she never used. No, she didn't know Dr. Casey well, but she knew his uncle, and she trusted him completely. The apple didn't seem to fall too far from the tree from what she could tell. And after all the trouble she'd been having figuring out how to make changes in her life, maybe she really did need time away to escape reality and determine what it was she really wanted.

The continuing education coursebook rested in Jackie's handbag. She had been excited to pick it up and browse through the course offerings. There were several courses that struck her fancy: cooking courses and craft courses and even a journaling course that sounded interesting. But it being nearly November, the fall courses had already begun. And the winter courses didn't start for another month. That left Jackie in limbo until then. Unless she did something else to get herself moving. Like take a road trip.

She had to discuss it with Mary. There was no way she could make this decision on her own. She needed someone else's rational thinking to help her figure out what to do.

Tuesday seemed an eternity away, but somehow Jackie made it. As she waited impatiently for Mary to arrive, she found she couldn't keep still. When Mary entered the room and glanced her way with a wave, Jackie's expression stopped her dead in her tracks.

"Are you okay, Jackie?"

"Um. I think so. I just really, really need to talk to you."

Mary glanced at her watch. "Well, we have a few minutes before the other members should be here. What's up?"

"I've been presented with an...opportunity, let's call it. And I don't know what to do about it."

"What kind of opportunity?"

Jackie filled Mary in and watched Mary's eyes grow wide.

"That seems kind of sudden, don't you think? What made him suddenly decide to take the trip now?"

"I don't know. We had both talked about making changes in our lives, but we were talking about little changes to get our feet wet at first. He shaved his beard, and I started looking into continuing education classes. Then suddenly he comes into the office, talks to his uncle for five minutes and springs this on me. I don't know what to do."

"Something must have happened. Something big. I don't think he would just suddenly decide to take over the practice and go on a road trip without something sending him over the edge. Maybe you should start with that. Ask him why now?"

"I could. But he'll still expect my answer, and I have no idea what to tell him."

"If you're not comfortable with the idea, then don't go. There's nothing forcing you to go. And even if he will be your future boss, he can't fire you for refusing to go on a recreational road trip with him. That would have me running to the labor board before the words even left his lips."

"I know. And my first inclination was to say 'no.' I didn't even think about the getting fired part. Or the future boss part. That just makes it more complicated."

"So your decision is made?"

"I don't know. I'm so confused. Like I said, my first inclination was to say 'no.' But the more I thought about it, the more I started thinking that maybe it was a good idea. Or at least not a bad idea. Maybe it would be good for me to get away. My life has always been so safe and predictable. Maybe I should just take a risk for once. Maybe little changes won't be enough to make me happy."

"You have a valid point. But is this the kind of risk you want to take?"

"Would I ever instigate this big a change on my own? Or have the guts to see it through?"

By the time book club was over, Jackie still hadn't made up her mind. Though Mary hadn't told her what to do, just talking over the situation solidified things in Jackie's mind. Despite her reservations, it was a great opportunity. When else would she do something like this? Probably never. If she didn't grab the bull by the horns now, maybe she would regret it for the rest of her life. The rest of her dull, meaningless, quiet, lonely life. It was a depressing thought.

But even if she decided to go with him, she needed to know why. Why now, why all of a sudden, and why take her with him?

Chapter 8

The rest of the week dragged. By the time Friday arrived, Jackie was staring at the clock every five minutes, wondering when Dr. Casey would show up. He arrived shortly before twelve, just as Jackie was preparing to leave for lunch.

"Excellent. I seem to have perfect timing," he said as he approached the window. He nodded toward her lunch bag. "I had hoped to catch you on your lunch break so we would have a chance to talk."

Jackie was usually the only one in the break room during lunch. The rest of the staff tended to go out to eat or run errands on their lunch breaks instead. Today was no exception. Jackie rested her lunch bag on the table and sat down. Dr. Casey pulled out the chair across from her.

"So have you given any thought to what I suggested?"

"I have. Quite a bit actually."

"And?"

"I have a question for you before I give you my answer."

"Okay." He leaned back in the chair and tucked his hands behind his head. It was a relaxed pose, but Jackie could see that he was actually nervous. Surprisingly, it put her more at ease.

"I just wondered why you made this sudden decision. We were talking about making small changes, and then you spring this on me. Why the sudden change of heart?"

Dr. Casey sighed and leaned forward again. "I'm not surprised you asked. I'm sure it did seem to come out of the blue." He paused a moment, as if formulating his thoughts. "The truth is, I was struggling with what to do. I had some decisions to make to determine which path I should take, so to speak. I thought making some small changes would help me get a better grasp on the big changes I knew would have to be dealt with. All I managed to do was get myself more confused." He paused again, glanced up briefly to meet Jackie's gaze, then looked down at the table. "You know the situation with my wife. I thought maybe we had a chance, that maybe our marriage was salvageable. One of the decisions I had to make was if I would fight for it. I decided to call her, to discuss it rationally and get her perspective."

When he didn't continue, Jackie couldn't help but ask "and?"

He sighed again. "And she made it abundantly clear that she does not want to work things out. Apparently I get no say in the matter, but either way my marriage is over. The papers were waiting at my uncle's house when I arrived last night."

"And that's why you decided to take over the practice here?"

He nodded. "In part. I had already been considering it. Uncle Bill can be very persuasive," he added with a half-smile. "But it was far from Pam, and she had never been keen on my having my own practice. When I found out we didn't have a chance, I figured maybe it was time to take that risk."

"And the road trip?"

"I've always wanted to take a road trip. A big one, like cross-country. But that was another thing Pam discouraged, so I never went. To be honest, I could really use a break to clear my head and get myself on track. With the timing of everything, I figured now might be my chance to finally hit the road, so to speak."

"So why take me with you?"

"Because I think you could use a break, too. I know how you don't like change, and maybe doing something out of the ordinary like this will help you. I don't know. It just seemed like the right thing to do."

Jackie unwrapped her sandwich, taking the time to process everything Dr. Casey had just said. It made sense, though it sounded in part like he was just running from things. But he had made the commitment to return, to take over the practice. Surely he wouldn't have done that if he didn't want to have a future, to create a life for himself? But what about her? Was his explanation compelling enough for her to give in to her temptation and go with him? What would she be coming back to?

He waited patiently while she ate her sandwich, for which she was grateful. This was not a decision she had come to lightly. He seemed to know that about her, that she took the time to really think things through before acting. She was cautious, perhaps overly so. But she was glad he accepted and respected it.

"Okay."

"Okay, what?"

"Okay, I'll go with you."

Dr. Casey grinned then and stood up. With a big step toward her side of the table, he leaned down and enveloped her in a hug. Jackie was startled, but he let go a moment later, and she was able to resume breathing.

"I'm so happy you've decided to go. I've got some great plans for us. For this trip we'll just stick with the east coast, but there's lots to see. I think we'll start with Maine and work our way down, since it'll be getting colder as we drive. Might as well drive somewhere warmer!"

He was so excited, Jackie couldn't help but laugh. But she had to stop him. "One thing at a time. There's something else I need to discuss with you."

Dr. Casey sat back down, but the grin was still plastered on his face. "Anything."

Jackie took a deep breath. This decision had been even harder. "When we come back from our little adventure, I won't be working for you."

His grin faded. "What do you mean? You've worked here for ten years. Where would you go?"

Jackie looked down at the table and played with the plastic wrap from her sandwich. "I haven't decided yet. I hoped I would kind of figure that out while we were gone."

"But why? Is it something I did?"

Jackie shook her head. Her eyes were starting to well up with tears, but she swallowed them back. "No. I just think all things considered, it would be awkward for us to work together. I decided that it was one thing or the other: take the road trip with you or work with you when you returned. I was tempted to just stay home and remain in my comfort zone, but I realized that I wouldn't get anywhere that way. I need to get out there, shake things up a bit. It scares the heck out of me, but I think it's something I need to do. So I decided to go with you. I have some money saved. I don't do anything after all, so there's nothing to spend my money on. I'll be fine for a while, even if I don't find something right away. I'd be happy to train my replacement, but I won't be coming back to work."

He cradled his head in his hands for a moment, then looked up at her again. "I'm sorry, Jackie."

"There's nothing to be sorry about. You've given me a wonderful opportunity that I'm nervous but excited to take. I just knew something had to give."

"You always have been practical."

Jackie shrugged. "It's served me well so far. I can only hope it continues to."

"Well, I must say I'm disappointed. I'm happy to have company on my trip, but I'll miss you when you've gone. The office won't be the same without you."

Tears were threatening again, but Jackie took a deep breath. "It's for the best."

"Then I guess I can't change your mind?"

She shook her head.

"We'd better have one hell of a trip then." He gave her another half-smile, but this one didn't quite reach his eyes.

Jackie tried to return the smile. "So when do we leave?"

Chapter 9

Arrangements were made with a temp agency, and Jackie spent the weekend packing. They had decided to leave Monday morning. They would be heading up to Maine to start, as per Dr. Casey's plan. The weather was already chilly, and Jackie could only hope they didn't get caught in bad weather during their drive. She hadn't heard word of snow yet, but upstate New York and northern New England definitely got hit harder than she was used to. Still, there was no way they could put the trip off until spring. The effect, the impact, would be lost by then. Jackie only hoped they would travel swiftly through the northern states before hitting the warmer climate of the south.

Jackie's thoughts and emotions were in constant upheaval. She alternated between being excited to explore states she had never visited and terrified at the risk she was taking. She had yet to determine which side would win out, but she refused to back out of the trip.

Despite that determination, her conversation with her mother the previous day floated back to her. Though she hadn't discussed her changes, there was always that question about what her mother would think about it all.

Jackie's mother was a firm believer in the traditional life: women ruled the roost. When Jackie expressed interest in going to college, her mother didn't hold her back, but she encouraged her to go into a profession that would be easy to leave once the husband and babies showed up. There was no room for a career-oriented passion. It had never been discussed, and any ideas Jackie had had were swallowed before they were even spoken. She had her life planned out, and there would be little deviation.

But what if she didn't like the plan? What if she grew bored? Lonely? What if the husband didn't magically appear like her mother expected? Then what? Would she be an old maid? Would she live the rest of her life following the same routines, punching in at the same job, greeting the same people?

As serious and straight-laced as Jackie could be, she didn't want to succumb to the idea that she couldn't have more. There had to be something more.

Despite the fact that they hadn't known each other long – and, until this drama, not very well – Jackie was grateful she had Mary to turn to. She was a great sounding board, and her experience in this area had proved invaluable. When Jackie called to let her know the final decision, Mary had been filled with concern and advice and had made Jackie promise to call with updates. So Jackie promised to call every other evening to let her know everything was okay.

Jackie's car was reliable, but older, so they decided to take Dr. Casey's car instead. When he pulled into her driveway Monday morning, Jackie's heart leapt into her throat. This was it. She could hardly believe she was actually going through with it. She scrambled around the house to make sure all the doors and windows were locked, though she had already checked them three times. Her insurance agent was aware she was going out of town. A trusted neighbor promised to check in periodically and water her plants. Her mail was being held. She had thought of everything but was convinced she had forgotten something. There had to be something she was missing. Why else would she feel like this?

She checked the front door four times before finally leaning back in Dr. Casey's car seat and trying to relax. She took a few deep breaths. "I'm sorry, Dr. Casey."

He laughed. "Now might be a good time to start calling me Paul."

Jackie blushed. "You have a good point." She turned to look at him, her head leaning against the headrest. "I don't know if I can do this."

He patted her knee and smiled at her. "Of course you can. You wouldn't have agreed to it if you couldn't."

She looked forward, then closed her eyes and swallowed. A moment later she nodded. "Okay. I'm ready."

Paul couldn't keep himself from grinning every time he looked over to his passenger's seat. Jackie looked terrified but determined, and he had to commend her for not letting her fears get the best of her. He made sure he drove extra carefully so as not to alarm her. He had already given her a copy of all the plans he had made, information on sites he considered visiting, hotels along the way and more. Anything he could think of that would make her feel more in control and more involved in what was going on.

Damn, he was glad she was there.

He hadn't expected to have such a strong reaction, but it was nice to not be on this adventure alone. And it wasn't just the fear of being alone with his thoughts. It was the knowledge that he would have someone to share this experience with, someone to laugh with or argue with or get lost with. It wouldn't have been nearly as much fun by himself. It was just a shame that she would be leaving him when the trip was over. Maybe if they became friends they could at least keep in touch. He could hope anyway.

The start of the trip was relatively quiet. The radio provided background music, but the conversation was limited to directions and food inquiries. Paul hoped the awkwardness would dissipate over time. He knew Jackie's nerves were tainting the atmosphere, but he didn't want to pressure her. He was sure in time she would relax and get used to his presence and the open road.

The scenery was beautiful, but he had known it would be. In the distance he could see mountains, and the trees everywhere he looked were decked out in their fall colors. It was perfect, peaceful. Riding in near silence, with nothing but the scenery to distract him, was soothing. He found his mind wandering, and for once he didn't seem to be focusing on Pam. He was just thinking about what lay around the next bend, and the sites they would see over the next couple of weeks.

By the time they stopped for lunch, Jackie seemed to be less tense, and Paul was grateful. "Feeling better?"

"A little." She gave him a tentative smile. "Sorry I'm so nervous."

"I don't blame you. I'm a little nervous myself."

"You don't seem nervous."

"Well, I guess I just hide it better. This is a big step for me, too, you know. At the very least I never planned any of our vacations. Pam was always the planner, and she had our itinerary planned out to the minute. It was kind of exciting to figure out where you and I would go and all that. But I admit I have no idea how long things are going to take us or even where we're going to stop for the night."

Jackie sighed. "I'm usually a planner, too. But I figured this trip might give me a little time to relax. Maybe it'll be good for both of us to have to fly by the seat of our pants for once." She smiled again. "We are looking for change, after all."

"That we are." He returned the smile.

The meal passed pleasantly. Conversation flowed much more smoothly than it had all day. It gave Paul hope that the trip would be as engaging as he had anticipated.

Jackie was starting to relax. She still had her reservations, and she definitely still had butterflies in her stomach, but Dr. Casey -- Paul -- was easy to get along with. He didn't pressure her or try to get her involved in conversation when she obviously wasn't ready. But she was glad to find that when she was ready, they had a lot to talk about. It gave her hope that maybe the trip wouldn't be as difficult as she had feared.

"So where do you think we should stop for the night?" Paul asked, nibbling on a french fry.

"You want to stop already?"

Paul laughed. "I take it you like being on the road."

"I just figured we'd want to get to Maine as quickly as possible."

Paul cocked his head at Jackie. "This isn't a race, Jackie. The whole point is to enjoy the trip, not try to make it through as quickly as possible."

Jackie blushed. "I know. I just worry about the weather. I don't want to get caught in Maine in the middle of a blizzard."

Paul glanced out the window, where blue skies and white puffy clouds waited for them. "I don't think we have to worry about that just yet. It's pretty nice out. And it's still early. I don't think we have to worry about snow yet."

"I'm sure you're right. I'll just be glad when we start hitting the warmer states."

"Did you want to bypass the northern states altogether?"

"No, no. We should see it all. Not really a tour of the east coast if we skip half of it," she added with a smile.

"I agree, but I want you to be comfortable."

She smiled again. "I'll be fine." He really was accommodating. But this was his trip, and she refused to spoil it for him, even if she did have her concerns. Besides, wasn't one of the reasons for taking this trip to let loose and shake things up a bit? She couldn't very well do that while still being overly cautious. It was time to relax and not worry so much. "So what did this plan of yours have us doing first?"

Paul shrugged. "I had some ideas, but nothing concrete. Vermont and New Hampshire are supposed to be beautiful. I thought we could just drive through and enjoy the scenery. I imagine the foliage will be nice there, too."

"I've always wanted to see New England in the fall."

"Well, then, we shall. Too bad it's not earlier. We could have picked apples and pumpkins."

"There's always next year." Jackie grinned. It was nice to dream anyway.

"Yes, there's always next year." Paul returned the grin. "I'm glad to hear you're not breaking off all contact, even if you are deserting me."

Jackie blushed. "I'm sorry. It probably wasn't fair of me to have made such a condition."

"Does this mean you're gonna work for me after all?"

She shook her head. "No. I'm just sorry it leaves you in the lurch."

"Oh."

He seemed disappointed, and she really was sorry that she was leaving him stranded. She was sure it couldn't be easy to take over a business like that and have to worry about hiring someone new right off the bat. But it would be too strange, too awkward, to work for him after being on the road with him for who knew how long.

She had no idea what she would do when she got back, though. The thought terrified her, actually, She was sure she could get another job in a doctor's office. Dr. Collins would probably give her a good reference. But there was an inkling of something in her belly that was making her think she'd like to do something different. She had worked in an office since she had graduated high school. Sixteen years. Her major in college had been business administration. Practical, responsible, guaranteed her a job. But it wasn't as if she was passionate about what she did. She was just good at it. But maybe it wasn't enough anymore.

"You're awfully quiet all of a sudden." Paul sipped his cola and looked at her with curiosity. "Everything okay?"

"Hmm? Oh, yeah. I was just thinking."

"I'm sorry. I didn't mean to pressure you about the job thing. It's entirely your decision."

"No, it's okay. I understand. It's probably not good to admit it to you of all people, but I have no idea what I'm going to do for a job once I leave."

"What do you want to do?"

Jackie shrugged. "If I knew that, I'd know what I was going to do." She gave him a crooked half-smile. "I'm hoping I'll get some inspiration on this trip."

"I hope so, too."

"Ready to go?"

"Sure."

They threw away their food wrappers and returned to the car. It really was a beautiful fall day, and Jackie couldn't help but close her eyes and tilt her head back to feel the cool breeze blow through her hair. Despite her nerves, it felt good to be somewhere different, enjoying the fresh air, not confined by a schedule or obligations. It was an unusual feeling of freedom. She had thought she wouldn't like it, but she found it exhilarating. She could only imagine how she would feel when their trip was over.

Silence fell once again when they were back on the road, but it was a companionable silence. Jackie seemed to be more at ease, and Paul found himself humming along to a song on the radio. Before he could stop himself, he was belting out the tune at the top of his lungs. To his surprise, Jackie joined in. They had found a radio station that specialized in songs from the eighties and nineties, and each song brought back memories. Ah, to be that young and carefree again. He found it fitting as a soundtrack for this trip.

Since there weren't really any specific sites they wanted to see on the way to Maine, Paul figured the trip would be relatively quick. They would probably stop for the night soon, and then tomorrow finish the trip to Maine. If they saw signs for anything interesting, they could always stop, but it was pleasant enough just enjoying the ride. Pleased with his course of action, Paul started looking for hotel signs. It was still early, but as he had told Jackie, they weren't in a race. There was no set time frame for this excursion; they could take as long as they wanted. Perhaps toward the end of the trip they would be tired, anxious to head home, but for now he would enjoy the freedom and joy of an unstructured schedule. Soon enough he would be back to the daily grind.

Just after they entered Vermont, Paul made the executive decision to pull into their welcome center. Might as well find out what Vermont really had to offer. He didn't know much about Vermont, but he knew two things: cheese and Ben & Jerry's. Surely every woman would want to sample at least one of those things. Jackie seemed game, so they browsed the racks of brochures.

"Hey, Jackie, feel like heading up north a bit?"

Jackie put down the brochure she was looking at and joined him. "What did you find?" He handed her the Cabot and Ben & Jerry's flyers. Jackie grinned. "Sounds good to me."

With a destination in mind, the trip was even more pleasant. There was a sense of anticipation in the air, an excitement that encouraged them to move just a little bit faster. And once they reached their destinations, they learned something new, enjoyed samples and found themselves just a little bit happier.

Precedent set, they made the decision to visit each visitor's center and see what the states had to offer. It would give them something to look forward to, without destroying the feeling that they were exploring rather than planning.

But New Hampshire would wait until tomorrow. For now, it was time to find a hotel and settle in for the night. While it wasn't late, it had been a busy day, and Paul was yawning. He wasn't used to so much driving in one day. So they located a hotel near the New Hampshire border and checked in. After bringing in their suitcases, they decided to meet in the hallway in an hour to discuss dinner.

Jackie rested her suitcase on the rack and kicked off her shoes. It had been an eventful day, and her emotions had been all over the place. It was hard to believe she was really here, in a different state, in a hotel room, separated from her kind-of boss by only a thin wall. It sounded indecent when she put it that way, and that made her nervous. What would other people think about her? She wasn't a rebel, or a bad girl. She was the sane, sensible, responsible one.

Jackie took a deep breath. They had had a nice day. There wasn't anything indecent about what they had done that day. Paul had been a perfect gentleman. They had explored a little, enjoyed some nice scenery, enjoyed each other's company. It was fine.

After her mental pep talk, Jackie began to relax. Yes, she was acting in an uncharacteristic manner, but that was what she had wanted. This was good for her. It was good for her to break out of her comfort zone and take chances. Change was good for her. It would break the monotony, the loneliness, the boredom. No one could tell her today had been normal!

Since she had some time before dinner, Jackie decided to check in with Mary before freshening up. If she had been nervous this morning, she was sure Mary had been even worse.

"Hello?"

"Hi, Mary. It's Jackie."

"Jackie! I'm so glad you called. Are you all right?"

Jackie couldn't help but laugh. "Of course I'm all right. Why wouldn't I be?"

"I don't know. I just kept picturing all these horrible scenarios in my head, and I couldn't help but think something bad was going to happen."

"Rest assured nothing bad has happened. Paul has been a gentleman, and we had a lovely day. We're in Vermont right now. We decided to explore a little and check out some cheese and ice cream."

"Ugh. Don't mention food to me. I haven't been able to keep anything down in weeks. But I'm glad you're having a good time."

"Definitely. I was really nervous this morning, but I'm doing better now."

"No more nerves?"

"Well, I'm still a little nervous. But things are going well so far, and I'm enjoying myself. It's an adjustment to say the least, but it's definitely broadening my horizons. And it's only just begun."

"That it has. I can't believe you'll be away for so long – and with a man you barely know."

"Me neither. But it feels right." Jackie's stomach did a little flip. "I am nervous about one thing, though."

"What's that?"

Jackie hadn't told Mary about her decision to leave her job when she returned, and she filled Mary in.

"I don't blame you."

Jackie closed her eyes and released a breath. "Really?" It felt good to have her feelings reinforced.

"Absolutely. That would just be strange, to have to work with him after this. I kind of wondered how that would work out for you."

"You don't think I'm nuts for not having a plan in place?"

"Well, it's not the most brilliant move, but you don't know how this trip is going to affect you. It would be a shame to have lined something up and then realized you don't want to do it anymore."

"Yeah. That's kind of what I was thinking. Not that I really had any time to line up another job. Things happened rather suddenly. But I'm already thinking I might want to try something different."

"No more doctor's offices?"

"Probably not."

"What are you thinking?"

"That's the problem. I don't really know yet."

"Well, keep me posted. It'll be interesting to see – or hear, anyway – this transformation. I'm really curious what's going to happen to you."

"Gee, thanks. You make it sound so appealing."

Mary laughed. "I know I worry a lot, but I think you may have made the right choice. I'm sure this trip is going to change you, make you look at the world a little differently. If you come out happier, then it'll definitely have been worth it."

They found a steakhouse not far from the hotel, and after a short wait were seated in a booth by the window. The day's events had been low-key and inexpensive, but over the course of the trip, things would add up. It was going to get expensive, and both wanted to be cautious, but they still wanted to enjoy themselves. So a compromise: they would enjoy nice dinners but quick lunches. And they wouldn't go overboard. Both of their futures were uncertain, and they couldn't afford to go crazy. Or, at least, any crazier than they had already gone. And if the money started dwindling, they would make sacrifices later on.

"So, New Hampshire tomorrow." Paul played with the wine in his glass, gazing at the deep red liquid as it swirled.

"Yup. And Maine."

"I was watching some TV before dinner."

"Okay."

"It's supposed to get colder. Make sure you dress warmly."

"Yes, Dad." Jackie grinned.

Paul had the grace to look bashful. "I'm sorry. I just wanted to give you a heads up."

"I know. Don't worry, I was so nervous before we started this trip that I think I packed everything in my closet. I've got clothes for all kinds of weather. I should be set."

"Good." He took a sip of his wine.

Their meals arrived shortly thereafter, and Paul cut into his steak. It looked delicious, but he found he couldn't enjoy it. He was afraid to tell Jackie the rest of what he found out.

Jackie looked over at his nearly-untouched plate. "Everything okay?"

Paul nodded, then took another sip of his wine. "Yeah."

Jackie cocked her eyebrows but returned to her meal. "This is delicious."

"I'm glad you're enjoying it." Paul took a small bite of his mashed potatoes.

After a moment Jackie put down her fork. "Okay, what's up?"

"What do you mean?"

"You seem distracted."

Paul sighed. "I know. I'm sorry. There was more to the weather forecast than the cold."

Jackie folded her hands in her lap, giving Paul her full attention. "Okay. What else?"

"It's still early to tell, but there's a storm brewing. They don't know if it'll be big, but it's got potential."

"Snow?"

"Yeah, a Nor'easter."

"Okay." Jackie swallowed and took a sip of her water. "So what do you want to do?"

"What do *you* want to do?"

Jackie looked up at him. "This is your trip, Paul."

"This is *our* trip, Jackie. Turning back might be the more logical approach, but I don't know if I can bring myself to do it without feeling cheated."

"Well, when are they talking about it hitting, if it does hit?"

"The weekend."

"Okay, so that gives us a few days to come up with a plan. We can still go to New Hampshire and Maine tomorrow. If the storm progresses, then we would still have enough time to turn around."

"Is that what you want to do?"

"No, but as you said, it's probably the more logical approach."

They ate in silence for a few minutes. After a while Jackie put her fork down again.

"I'm tired of being logical."

Paul grinned. "Me, too."

"So what do we do?"

"Keep going?"

Jackie giggled. "Would we be crazy to?"

"Probably."

"Mary would worry."

"Who's Mary?"

"A friend. She's been my inspiration."

"Would that make you feel bad?"

"Probably."

"I don't want you to feel bad."

"I think Mary would understand."

"Are you sure?"

"Yeah."

"Okay."

There was silence for a moment as they grinned at each other.

"So are we really doing this?" Paul broke the silence.

"I think we are."

"All right, then." He raised his glass. "Let's make a toast, then. To our insanity and poor sense, and hoping they steer us well."

Jackie laughed. "Or at least give us a heck of an adventure on the way down."

They clinked glasses and resumed their dinners, chatting animatedly. Paul was glad Jackie had been on the same page as he was, even if they both lived to regret it. But when it came to adventure, logic was overrated. If they got stuck in the storm and had to wait it out, so what? They weren't in a hurry. They had nowhere specific to be. They would just keep an eye on things and not do anything too risky. If nothing else, it would make a great story when they got back.

Jackie lay on her back in bed that evening, staring at the ceiling. She was having difficulty falling asleep, and her mind kept drifting back to their conversation at dinner. It was easy to be brave with Paul. She thought some of his craziness must be rubbing off on her. But when she was alone with her thoughts, she didn't know if she had the courage to shrug off logic and practicality. Were they nuts for going forward? Should they turn back while they could? Just the thought gave Jackie a hollow feeling in the pit of her stomach. She didn't want to go back. She had just been starting to feel carefree. She didn't want to go back to the dull schedule of her life.

Anyway, she couldn't tell Paul she had changed her mind. That wouldn't be fair to him. And what was the worst that could happen, anyway? They would get stuck for a couple of days. Storms passed. When the roads were clear, they would proceed. No problem. They would just keep an eye on things and stop at a hotel when things really got going. Easy as pie.

Chapter 10

There was a definite chill in the air Tuesday morning. The sky was still blue, but it was easy to imagine thick clouds moving in. Jackie shuddered and pulled her coat tighter. She knew at least part of it was from being farther north, but knowing that there might be snow on the way didn't help, either.

Much of what interested them was closed for the season, so they opted to just enjoy the scenery and drive through the White Mountains area. Despite their enthusiasm the night before, both were quiet, distracted. Jackie wondered if Paul had the same concerns as she did. Were they crazy for doing this? Was that half the fun, or a foolish idea?

The views were beautiful. There was no denying that New Hampshire held appeal in terms of that. But Jackie found she wasn't quite able to enjoy it. By the time they reached Maine, she was starting to get depressed. Looking over at Paul, with his tense jaw, she thought he might be feeling the same way.

"Paul?"

"Hmm?" His eyes didn't veer from the road, until she didn't respond, then he glanced her way before resuming his rigid pose. "What's up?"

"Do you think we're making a mistake?"

The tension seemed to pour out of him, and his shoulders fell several inches. "I don't know."

"I want us to enjoy this trip, but I'm afraid we're going to regret it."

"I know. Me, too."

"So what do we do?"

"I don't know. It may sound childish, but I don't want to go back."

"Me, neither." Jackie wrung her hands in her lap.

Paul glanced at her again. After a few minutes of silence, he took the nearest exit. There were several fast food places around, and he pulled into the parking lot of one and parked the car. Neither spoke.

"The storm's coming from the south, though right now it's kind of off the coast. If we were to head back now, we should be fine. I doubt we'd get much. The farther east we go, the greater the chance we'll get hit. They expect it to make landfall on the coast of Massachusetts and Southern Maine."

"So right where we're headed next."

"Pretty much. It's still early in the year, so we may not get hit too badly. It might be more rain and wind than anything. But if it's cold enough..."

Jackie sighed and looked out the window. "Maybe we should just find a place to stop and kind of camp out for a while."

"If it's bad, though, who knows how long we'll be stuck."

She looked back at him. "I can think of worse things."

He grinned. "Like going home?"

She returned the smile, though she wasn't quite calm yet. "Yeah."

"Well, we still have a few days. Supposedly. It can be hard to tell. Do you want to stop in Maine, or try to make it through Massachusetts, into Rhode Island or Connecticut? We might miss a lot of the storm then."

"I'd hate to fly through the states because we're trying to beat a storm. And if we don't end up beating it, we could get stuck."

"True. So Maine or Massachusetts?"

"Maybe we could stop for the night in Maine, then tomorrow we can head into Massachusetts and stop near Boston or something. That way if we end up having to camp out for a few days, there should be plenty to do."

Paul nodded. "Sounds like a plan."

"So much for not planning this trip, huh?" Jackie gave him a half-smile.

"I guess it can't be avoided sometimes," he responded with a smile of his own.

They took their time over lunch. Since they had already reached Maine, there wasn't a rush to get anywhere specific. They opted for enjoying more scenery.

They would head east to the coast, check out the beaches and shops near Freeport, then head south before stopping. It was a leisurely trip, and though they were still anxious over the threat of snow, they were going to try and make the best of what they had.

They reached Boston late morning on Wednesday. They found a reasonable hotel on the outskirts, then decided to take the T into the city to explore. Bundled up against the cold air they wandered the Freedom Trail and checked out Faneuil Hall before heading to Quincy Market for a late lunch. By the time they were finished, clouds had moved into the area, enhancing the cool temperatures and adding to the feeling of snow. Paul wouldn't be surprised if the first flakes fell before nightfall.

It was peaceful walking through the market with Jackie. The crowds weren't large since it was the middle of the week and the holiday shopping season hadn't officially begun. They checked out the unique items at the different carts, meandered into the stores along the edge. Jackie picked up a couple of small things for holiday gifts, which she tucked into her purse.

Paul couldn't even think about Christmas yet. He had no idea what the holiday would bring this year. Usually he and Pam would set up a tree a week or so beforehand, just in time to host a holiday party. Their friends and coworkers would flood the house, sipping on eggnog and avoiding the mistletoe. Christmas Day was spent opening gifts to each other before heading to his parents' house for lunch. Pam's parents lived in California, and they didn't speak much. Pam would usually call at some point to wish her parents a happy holiday, but that was about it. Gifts would have been sent out weeks before.

This year would definitely be different, though he was grateful he at least had Uncle Bill to keep him company. Paul didn't know where he'd be living yet. He didn't want to impose on Uncle Bill for much longer, but he got the feeling Bill liked having him around. It must be a nice change to a silent, empty house. But no matter where Paul ended up, he was sure he would still visit his parents. Uncle

Bill usually made an appearance anyway, so it would be like one big, happy family, just without Pam. He wondered what Jackie did for the holiday.

As they strolled along the shops, Paul was tempted to take her hand in his. It was so comfortable walking with her like this. The entire situation was less than ideal, but she had met it head-on and come up with a plan that made things bearable, even pleasant. He could only imagine how Pam would have reacted. Pam didn't like things to mess up her schedule. She would have refused to accept the possibility of a snowstorm. Or insisted he was crazy for having scheduled such an outing without first checking the long-term forecast. As if he were responsible. Of course if she were here, she would have planned out the entire trip, and checked the long-term forecast, so they likely wouldn't have been in this predicament in the first place.

Somehow, though, he couldn't make himself regret it. Especially when the first flakes fell and Jackie's eyes lit up like a child's. So what if they got hit with a little storm? Maybe it would be a blessing in disguise.

Jackie loved snow. And it seemed the perfect ending to a day filled with simple pleasures and holiday shopping. When Paul slipped his hand over hers, she only turned to him and smiled, her joy permeating from every pore. Yes, it was scary when she thought that this light flurry could turn into a potential blizzard, but for now she would enjoy the moment. And so she and Paul walked hand in hand around the market until they decided they should head back to the hotel.

They had selected a hotel that was a little pricier than some of the others they could have selected, but it had a restaurant on the main level. Their reasoning was that peace of mind was a lot better than a cheaper price tag, especially if the weather got really bad, and they couldn't leave the hotel. They wouldn't want to have to worry about finding food in a blizzard. They had also opted for a suite instead of 2 single rooms. That way they could each have their own privacy and space, but there would be a common area for them to lounge in to prevent boredom and loneliness. It seemed practicality had not deserted them after all.

They dined at the hotel restaurant before heading back up to the room. While out they had picked up a deck of cards to help the time pass, though the TV boasted movies and a large selection of channels, as well. As such they decided to spend the dwindling evening hours playing cards as they watched the snow fall.

The snow was still limited to a flurry, dusting the pavement in a thin layer of white. Turning on the news, though, informed them that the storm was building momentum and would likely hit them sometime the following afternoon. It would be a long night and day, but they were confident they could make it through.

Jackie was glad she wasn't here alone. The thought of being stranded alone in a blizzard made her shiver, and it was more than the thought of cold. She wasn't a brave person, and she certainly wouldn't have had the courage to face the impending obstacles alone. But with Paul she felt safe, brave, more able to handle whatever was thrown her way. When they decided to retire for the night, and she bid him farewell, she closed the door to her room and gazed at the empty bed. Part of her wished he could stay with her, that he would just lie beside her so she wouldn't feel so alone.

It was an alarming thought, and one she tried anxiously to push away. While she certainly wasn't opposed to the idea of being with a man, in a relationship, comforted in masculine arms, it certainly couldn't be with Paul! Though at this point she could hardly argue that she didn't know him very well, that didn't change the fact that he was still legally married, and therefore off-limits. Add to that the complicated working relationship, and there was no way she could even consider crossing that line. It was impossible. And entertaining any feelings that led her down that path would bring her nothing but heartache and frustration. Better to nip them in the bud. Besides, any feelings she may or may not have at this point were likely brought on by the intimacy thrust upon them by circumstance, not anything real.

It wasn't until she was getting ready for bed that she realized she hadn't called Mary. She toyed with the idea of waiting until the morning, but realized that that would only cause Mary to worry even more. Though it was getting late, it was better to set both their minds at ease.

Mary answered after one ring, as though sitting by the phone. "Hello?"

"Hi, Mary."

"Jackie! I was worried when I didn't hear from you."

"I'm sorry."

"No, it's okay. I know you can take care of yourself, and you probably just lost track of time and all that. I just heard about the snowstorm, and I thought about you. Where are you?"

"Boston."

"Massachusetts?"

Jackie laughed. "Do you know another Boston?"

"No, I mean, I know. But seriously? You're in Massachusetts? That's where the blizzard's supposed to hit."

"I know. We've thought it all through. We're in a hotel. The hotel has a restaurant. We figure we'll stay here until the storm passes, then move on. We're being smart. No reason to worry."

"I had hoped you would head home."

"The thought crossed our minds. But we were too excited to go on to turn back. Besides, that wouldn't have solved anything, not really. We would have been too disappointed."

"I know. I'm sure you're right. You're smart. You won't do anything too stupid. I think it's just my hormones. I get all wound up over everything."

"I don't blame you. You're just gearing up for when you're a mommy."

Jackie could practically hear Mary smiling. "I can't wait."

"I know. And you're going to be a great mom."

"Thanks, Jackie."

"Well, I just wanted to check in. It's late. I should probably head to bed, even though there's no reason to get up early tomorrow."

"Well, stay safe."

"We will."

"Good night."

"G'night."

Jackie disconnected the call and crawled into bed. She couldn't help but smile. Mary was so worried about what happened to her, and yet Mary had been the one to marry a man she barely knew. Were the tables reversed, however, Jackie was sure she would behave the same way.

Jackie yawned and turned off the light. Through the window on one side of the room she could still see fluffy white flakes floating down to earth. It was peaceful, and Jackie's eyes drifted shut.

Paul was sitting in the common area, reading the complementary paper, when Jackie entered, still stifling a yawn. They were both dressed and ready to go, but there wasn't really anywhere to go. The snow was falling down harder now, and traffic was sluggish. Best to just ride out the storm.

"I thought we'd go downstairs and get some breakfast. Are you hungry?"

Jackie nodded, stifling another yawn. "Sure. Let me just grab my shoes."

"Did you not sleep well?" Paul had gathered that Jackie was a morning person. It surprised him that she would be barely awake at 8 in the morning.

"I slept fine. Just some strange dreams."

"Oh. Okay. Well if you're tired later, you can always take a nap. I don't think we'll be doing much today anyway."

They headed down to the breakfast buffet and helped themselves to heaping portions. As they lingered over coffee, Paul began to wonder what they would do all day. Though there were activities within walking distance, he doubted they would want to venture far. Yet they would need something to pass the time.

"So what do you want to do today?" The question came from Jackie, and Paul had no answer.

"I have no idea."

"Hmm. Do you think it's too bad outside to go for a walk?"

"We'd have to check. If you want to go out, though, we should probably get our coats."

"Yeah. And I'm feeling kind of lazy." She grinned at him.

"Me, too."

"I think I'd get bored just sitting in the room, though."

Paul sighed. "Me, too."

"Well, even if I'm feeling lazy, I think I'm going to grab my coat and venture outside. At the very least I need to work off all this food."

"All right. I'll join you. But if it's really bad out, we're turning around."

"Deal."

Paul had never even considered taking a walk in the snow with anyone else. Voluntarily going outside, getting wet and cold? No, thank you. But with Jackie he almost looked forward to it. It was another new experience, another memory. And if there was one thing he had learned so far on this trip, it was that he enjoyed Jackie's company. He could only imagine what the rest of the trip held.

They bundled up against the cold and stepped out into the swirling snow. It was beautiful, peaceful. Every sound was muffled. It was easy to pretend they were in the middle of nowhere, with nothing but the wind and snow for company. But they weren't the only crazy ones out and about, and they saw the occasional passerby battling the storm.

Some of the shops and restaurants were closed due to the weather. Along the way, however, they came across a café and bakery and decided to pick up some treats for later that afternoon. They sat at a table for a little while and watched the world go by. He was so used to constantly moving that the simple act of sitting was taking some adjusting. He found he rather liked it, though it was taking his mind longer to catch up than his body. His mind was still planning ahead, plotting their next steps, though they really had no way of knowing when they would be able to move on.

It ended up being a low-key day, as they expected it would. Paul found that even though they hadn't done much, he was exhausted. It didn't surprise him that Jackie fell asleep on the sofa while they were watching a movie. He debated if he should wake her or let her sleep. Not knowing the condition of the sofa, he decided it was probably better for her if she moved to the bedroom. He didn't want her to have a backache the next day.

Nudging her only elicited soft murmurs that made him grin. He shook her a little harder, then harder until her eyes blinked open. She smiled at him with a sleepy look in her half-closed eyes.

He couldn't help it. She looked so soft, so peaceful. He leaned forward to touch her lips with his, then pulled back as though burned. What was he thinking? He could only hope fatigue had clouded his brain.

Jackie sat up abruptly, seemingly fully awake now. "What was that for?"

"I'm sorry. I didn't mean to."

They sat and stared at each other for a moment until Paul looked away.

"You fell asleep," he finally said, still unable to look at her. "I didn't want you to get a backache."

"Thank you. I'll go to bed now." She got up stiffly and entered her bedroom without another word. A moment later he heard the door close and lock.

With a sigh, Paul stood up. What had he been thinking? Things were complicated enough without him throwing careless actions into the mix. And why had he done it anyway? Was he attracted to her? Yes, he enjoyed spending time with her. She had definitely made the trip more enjoyable thus far. But that didn't mean anything. That meant only that they could be friends, nothing more. He was married, for crying out loud! Even if his marriage was doomed, the paperwork had not even been filed, never mind legalized. If nothing else, Jackie was not the kind of woman who would have any kind of relationship with a married man. And he was not the kind of man who would put her in that position.

So what was that all about? Paul ran his fingers through his hair, disgusted with himself. After a moment he proceeded into his own bedroom and closed and locked the door. He could only hope that Jackie would forgive him for his lapse in judgment.

Jackie went through the motions of getting ready for bed, but the moment she was lying down, any thoughts of sleeping went out the window. Why did he do that? The look in his eyes had been so tender, so thoughtful. Looking up at him in her half-asleep haze, she had thought he was beautiful. But the minute his lips touched hers, reality set in. What had happened could certainly not be repeated. If he didn't think so, then she did. And she would just have to take precautions to ensure it didn't happen again. They had been having a perfectly pleasant time. There was no reason to ruin it now.

Jackie sighed and rolled over. It was going to be a long night.

Chapter 11

Paul was already up and reading the newspaper when Jackie entered the common area. She had finally fallen asleep at some point around midnight, and while she had slept later than usual, she was still exhausted.

"Hi." Paul greeted her quietly, almost shyly.

"Hi." She didn't know how to act, what to say. Had she imagined the whole thing? She didn't think so. But she didn't want it to affect their relationship – or lack thereof. They still had a long trip ahead of them. "Did you want to go down to breakfast?"

"Sure."

They ventured downstairs in silence. Paul seemed as reluctant to say anything as she was. Gone was the comfortable banter they had gotten used to sharing.

It wasn't until they were seated with their plates that Paul broke the silence.

"Look, Jackie, I'm sorry about last night."

Jackie poked her eggs with a fork and sighed before looking up at him.

"I know things are awkward now, and I hate that. It was a stupid impulse, and I regret it."

Jackie nodded. "Okay."

"Okay? We're okay?"

"Of course we're okay." She gave him a small smile. At least she hadn't been the only one who realized it was a mistake.

"Good." Paul relaxed noticeably in his chair. A moment later he picked up his fork and began eating.

Jackie gazed out the window. The snow seemed to be dwindling. Now it was mixed in with rain. Today would probably be a bust as well, but by tomorrow she hoped they would be back on the road. They interacted better when they were on the road. There weren't awkward moments to fill, bored hours to dread. On the road they were partners on a mission.

But they still had today to get through.

"So what should we do today? The weather seems to be getting better, but I'm sure the roads are still a mess." She turned back toward Paul.

He swallowed and glanced out the window. "Well, we could always take the T somewhere. Even if we don't want to drive, we can go somewhere, get out of the hotel. I'm sure places will be open today."

"Sounds good."

They ended up heading to the science center, and the day passed without further mention of the previous evening. Jackie was grateful. She just hoped it wouldn't rear its ugly head at some point during their trip. They had to put it behind them.

The fact that she was still thinking about it as she got ready for bed, however, did not bode well. She really had to forget it. It had been a mistake. Paul admitted it himself. And she certainly couldn't go around harboring feelings for the man given the circumstances. And she didn't even have feelings for him! Hadn't she just assured herself of that the other night?

With a sigh, Jackie sat on the bed and picked up the phone. She had to check in with Mary anyway. Maybe Mary would be able to offer some insight.

"Hey, Jackie. How's it going?"

Jackie couldn't conceal another sigh.

"That bad, huh?"

"No, it's not bad. We had a very pleasant day, actually. We should be able to hit the road again tomorrow."

"I'm glad to hear it. I take it the storm wasn't too bad."

"I think it helped that we're so close to the shore. It ended up turning into rain."

"That's good."

"Yeah."

"So why the sigh?"

"Something happened."

Jackie could practically hear Mary sit up straighter. "What happened?"

"Well, yesterday was a pretty boring day, and we ended up just hanging out a lot of it. Last night we were watching a movie on TV, and I ended up falling asleep. Paul woke me up to go to bed so I wouldn't get a backache."

"That was nice of him."

"Yeah."

"But?"

Jackie sighed again. "But after he woke me up, he kissed me."

"Uh oh."

"Exactly."

"Did you want him to kiss you?"

Jackie thought for a moment. Did she want Paul to kiss her? In a perfect world, would she want to be with him? "I don't know. I was half asleep. I wasn't exactly thinking straight. And things are so complicated right now, I don't think it was a smart idea."

"Agreed. But sometimes you can't help how you feel."

"I don't think I have feelings for him, though. I like him as a friend, but anything more is just not possible right now. And I don't even know if I want it to be possible. I'm trying to get myself on track. Not that I would mind being in a relationship, but I don't think a relationship with Paul is a good idea."

"Okay. So what did he do afterward?"

"Well, this morning he apologized, said that it was a mistake."

"Which you agree to."

"Yes."

"Then what's the problem?"

"Well, it made things awkward, for one. And I can't stop thinking about it, for two."

"So you *do* have feelings for him!"

"No, I don't. I just don't know what to do about it."

"Why do you have to do anything? You both agree it was a mistake. Are things still awkward?"

"No, they seem to be okay right now. I'm just afraid that once we're back on the road, without distractions, that it'll get awkward again."

"Well, you won't know that until you try."

"I know."

"Try not to let it bother you. I know it's hard, but sometimes obsessing about something just makes it worse. It's best to just put it out of your mind and focus on other things."

"I'll try."

"That's all you can do."

Paul didn't mean to overhear, but he couldn't help it. Okay, maybe he could. But when he turned off the TV, he heard Jackie say his name, and he just had to listen. He knew she was talking to her friend Mary, and he was dying to know just once what she was thinking. While she wasn't exactly cryptic, she did have a tendency to weigh her words carefully, and it was hard to get a feel for what she was actually feeling.

It pained him that he had put her in such an awkward position. Again, he kicked himself for acting on impulse. Why couldn't he think things through like Jackie did? And while he didn't want to bring it up again, she was obviously still thinking about it, so would it be bad for him to discuss it with her? Try to find a way to make it up to her?

Maybe he could give her free reins on their plans one day. They could do just what she wanted to do. She could even pick the day. Would she see right through him? Maybe. But he didn't care. He just wanted her to be happy.

He paused at that thought. Her happiness mattered to him. Like a friend, right? He just cared for her as a friend. And yet something she had said struck a nerve with him. She didn't have feelings for him. A relationship with him wasn't a good idea. While he didn't disagree, something about that bothered him. Did he want her to have feelings for him? Did he have feelings for her?

This was ridiculous! The whole situation was ridiculous. They were adults. They should be able to discuss this like adults. But how could they discuss it if he didn't even know how he felt?

Paul tossed the remote on the coffee table and went to his room. He was done eavesdropping. It hadn't helped him one bit. If anything, it made him even more agitated. Now he had more to think about, more to worry about.

This road trip was supposed to clear his head, and all it had done so far was blur things even more.

Chapter 12

"I want to help you."

Jackie nearly spit out her orange juice. "With what?"

They were enjoying a final breakfast at the hotel before hitting the road.

"I know you wanted to figure some things out on this trip, like what you wanted to do for a living. I want to help you figure it out."

Jackie cocked her head to one side and examined Paul. She guessed he was still feeling guilty about the kiss. "There's really no need. I'm capable of figuring it out on my own."

"I know you're capable. You're one of the most capable people I know. But everyone can use a little help sometimes. I thought we could maybe do some activities you want to do, that you're interested in. Maybe they'll spark some ideas."

"Okay..." She wasn't sure how to respond. She didn't want to take over their trip. It was actually his trip, and she was just a passenger along for the ride. It wouldn't be fair for her to dictate what they did and where they went. "But only once in a while. We have to do things you want to do, too."

Paul nodded. "Agreed. Maybe we can alternate things we want to do or something."

"Okay."

"So we'll be hitting the road again today. I figure we'll probably head to Rhode Island and Connecticut. Was there anything in particular you wanted to do there?"

Jackie shrugged. "I don't know what they have to offer. Are we ditching our game plan of checking out welcome centers?"

"No, we can still do that. I just didn't know if there was anything in particular you had in mind."

"No, nothing."

"Okay. Then we'll just check out the welcome centers." He smiled then, and Jackie couldn't help but give him a funny look. He was acting a little strange. He was being even more accommodating than usual, and she didn't know how to react.

Despite her concerns, the ride started off peacefully. They headed south down the eastern edge of Massachusetts, then cut across the coast of Rhode Island. The roads were still a little messy in some spots, but for the most part they had no trouble. They drove by the Newport mansions and stopped for a bite to eat at one of the many seafood restaurants lining the tourist area of the coast before moving on into Connecticut.

They were relatively quiet during the ride, but it was a somewhat companionable silence. They each seemed to have a lot to think about. By the time they stopped at Connecticut's welcome center, they both seemed to be more at ease, with just a little of the awkwardness gone.

"Feel like trying your luck?" Paul held up a flyer for Foxwoods casino.

"I've never gambled before." Jackie was somewhat shy to admit it, but it had never been a priority for her.

"Never?"

Jackie shook her head.

"That's it. We're going." He tucked the flyer in his pocket and reached for the Mohegan Sun casino ad as well.

"Um."

Paul looked up at her. "What?"

"Do you think that's a good idea? We still have a long way to go, and I don't want to waste all of my money at a casino."

"We won't stay long. But you've got to at least give it a shot. Plus it says here they have shops and restaurants and entertainment, too. Maybe we can spend the rest of the day there and then find a place to stay."

"Okay. But I'm not spending a lot."

"No problem."

They followed signs to the casinos and pulled into the driveway for Foxwoods.

"Wow, it's packed." Jackie looked around in amazement at all the cars filling the parking garage and the path leading into it. Even the valet parking area was filled.

"Well, it is a weekend."

"Yeah, but this is insane."

"Did you want to turn around?"

Jackie turned to look at Paul. It was tempting. She hadn't been too keen on this excursion to begin with. But she had to break out of her comfort zone. "No, it's okay."

They made their way to the top level of the parking garage, then entered the casino. It took only minutes to discover why it was so crowded.

"There's an event going on." Paul commented, nodding at the clusters of people.

Jackie was the first to see a sign. "It's a food and wine festival."

"Cool."

Jackie laughed. "Let's check it out."

They made their way to an information kiosk and were handed a brochure for the weekend's events.

"Wow, there are a bunch of famous people here. I bet the food is incredible."

"Did you want to go?"

Jackie nibbled on her lower lip. "It's pretty pricey."

"Yeah, but you're getting food and wine. This can be our nice dinner for today."

Jackie shot him a look. "It's more expensive than a nice dinner would cost. Look at the prices." She handed Paul the brochure.

"Oh. Hmm. Well, I still think we should do it."

"Why?"

"Because I haven't seen you so excited about something since we started this trip. And if it means that much to you, we should do it."

She was tempted. She would be lying if she said she wasn't. But was it worth it? She wasn't one to indulge. She was the practical one, the logical one. And it didn't make sense to spend over a hundred dollars when they could just as easily walk around for a few hours then spend considerably less on dinner. Still...

She continued to gaze at the pamphlet, even after Paul had started walking. She followed him blindly until he stopped again. Then she looked up to find them standing in line.

"Paul, what are we doing?"

"We're buying tickets."

"I don't know. I don't think we should."

"This trip isn't about what we should do. It's about experiencing life. And that's what we're doing."

She let him steer her through the line, even handed over her debit card to buy her admission ticket. It was as if she were in a daze, incapable of making a decision on her own. But when she held the ticket in her hand, she couldn't help but grin.

Paul grinned back. "Okay, let's do this."

They spent the next three hours wandering the different booths, sampling food, sipping wine, and chatting with chefs and connoisseurs.

Paul watched Jackie as they made their way around the Grand Ballroom. He had never seen her so animated, so excited. She savored each bite, commented on the wine pairings and asked intelligent questions. It was amazing to watch.

When the event was over, Paul steered her out into the crowded hallway. They managed to find an empty bench and sat down, resting their tired feet and letting their stomachs settle.

"Did you enjoy that?" Paul turned to find Jackie with her eyes closed, taking a deep breath. "Are you okay?"

"That was incredible."

He grinned. "So you don't regret doing it?"

Jackie shook her head. "I might later, but right now, no way."

"I'm glad to hear it. You seemed to have a good time."

"I did." She turned to Paul and opened her eyes. "Thanks for pushing me."

"No problem."

They sat in silence for a few moments, watching the crowds of people pass.

"You seem to have a real interest in food."

Jackie shrugged. "I guess." But a slight blush was creeping up her neck.

"It's nothing to be embarrassed about. I was actually thinking how great that was, to have a passion for something. Maybe it's something you should look into. You know, for your job after you leave me."

Jackie looked down at her hands. "I've thought about taking some cooking classes, but I don't know who I would cook for. I live alone, and I don't think I would be very good at throwing dinner parties."

"It doesn't have to be a party. You can just invite a friend or two over for dinner. I'm sure you'd get plenty of takers. With the interest you've shown, you're probably a natural in the kitchen."

"I don't know about that." Jackie's face was still red, and she refused to look at Paul. "I don't have any training. My mom taught me to cook, but nothing fancy."

"Hey, food doesn't have to be fancy to taste good."

"I know."

"Well, it's something to think about anyway." Paul stood up and stretched. While he wanted to give Jackie food for thought -- no pun intended -- he didn't want to embarrass her too much. "Now it's time to show you how to gamble."

Jackie shook her head. "No way. I spent too much today as it is."

"Then I'll treat. Not much, just twenty bucks. At least give the slots a try. There's nothing to them."

Jackie looked across the hallway, where one of the casinos beckoned. Even Paul had to admit the flashing lights and bells were tempting, and he wasn't much of a gambler himself.

"Okay. Just twenty." She reached into her purse to pull out a bill. Paul put a hand on her arm.

"Uh uh. My treat, I said. I pushed you into the food thing. And I'm pushing you into this. The least I can do is give you a twenty to play with."

Jackie didn't want to agree, he could tell. But she finally acquiesced, and Paul led her into the casino.

The noise was almost deafening, but at the same time it was exhilarating. The possibility to walk out with considerably more than they started with was appealing, though he knew it was far more likely for them to walk out empty-handed.

They managed to find two vacant machines and sat down. Paul inserted a twenty into Jackie's machine and gave her pointers on how to bet. Then he turned to his own machine and inserted another twenty.

He spun his reels half-heartedly, much more interested in watching Jackie's experience. He grinned as she squealed in excitement. It appeared she was having what could only be called "beginner's luck."

It was a shame, really, that the coins didn't come out of the machine anymore. In Paul's humble opinion, it had been a lot more exciting to hear the clatter of coins falling into the metal bin. But they were on the penny slots, so he supposed that would be a lot of coin to deal with. And it was a lot easier to hold back if you had a ticket in your hand instead of a bucket of coins.

It was nearly an hour before Jackie was willing to cash in said ticket. Despite her reluctance, she was all smiles walking away.

"I'm paying you back."

"Excuse me?" Paul led her toward the cashier so she could cash in her ticket.

"I'm paying you back."

"There's no need for that."

"Stop arguing with me." But she was still smiling. "I won more than enough to cover the initial investment. I almost paid for my food festival ticket!"

"Did you have a good time?"

"I did. But I can see how people can get addicted. It's easy to get wrapped up and lose track of time. And it's tempting to want to keep going, to keep building my winnings."

"We don't have to stop yet if you don't want to. You seem to be on a winning streak."

Jackie shook her head. "That's how you get into trouble. Besides, I'm tired. We've had a long day."

"Yes we have." Paul was amazed at her self-control. If it had been him with the hundred dollar ticket, he would be slipping it into the closest machine. But he supposed that was why he was walking away broke and she was walking away a winner. "So what do you want to do now? Are you hungry?"

Jackie groaned. "I'm still full from the festival." She checked her watch. "It's still relatively early. We could grab something later?"

"That's fine."

"Are you sure? If you're hungry, we can go somewhere now."

Paul smiled at her. "Jackie, it's fine. I'm fine."

"Okay." She handed over her ticket to the cashier, and a moment later they were heading out of the casino.

"Did you want to walk around a bit or hit the road and find a hotel for the night?"

"We can walk around for a little bit. I don't know how long I'll be able to keep going, though." She stifled a yawn. "It'll probably have to be an early night."

"Not a problem. I'm tired myself."

They spent about an hour walking around the shops before making their way back to the parking garage.

It had been a busy day, Jackie mused as she nestled into the car seat. She was exhausted. But it had been wonderful. It had been the icing on the cake that she had won at her first attempt at gambling. It made her feel a little less guilty for splurging on the food and wine festival. But even if she hadn't won, it would have been worth it. The food...and the chefs. She couldn't have asked for a better day.

"Thank you," she said, turning to face Paul.

He glanced her way before backing out of the parking space. "For what?"

"For indulging me."

"I told you we would do things you wanted to do."

"I know. But this was really your trip, your vacation. I shouldn't be hijacking it."

"You didn't hijack it. I had a good time, too. And it takes a little of the pressure off if you're coming up with some of the activities, too. It's nice to share the responsibility and the fun."

"I'm glad you had a good time, too. Did you enjoy the food?"

"It was delicious. Of course there were some things I liked more than others, but it was all good."

"Mmm...me, too. And so many of the chefs were down to earth. Well, the ones who weren't full of themselves, anyway."

Paul laughed. "Yeah, there were plenty of those, too."

Jackie sighed. Her thoughts drifted back to their conversation after the festival, before they tackled the slots. What would it be like to be one of those chefs? To have a TV show or travel the world cooking for people. You would have to have amazing confidence. There was no time for self-doubt if you were constantly bombarded with the public and its expectations. You just had to know your stuff and put it out there. It was a scary thought.

At the same time, though, it would be incredible to share your ability with the world. What would it feel like to make something and have someone else enjoy it as she had enjoyed what she tried today? The sense of pride, of fulfillment, would likely be worth any fear or awkwardness.

Maybe it was time to try her hand at it...

Chapter 13

The following day dawned bright and cool. It would be an awkward limbo-type day. Their next destination would be New York City, and they wanted to spend a full day there. But after the excitement of the previous day, they were too exhausted to make an early start. So they opted to sleep in a little and finish checking out Connecticut before heading into New York. It would delay them a little, but since they had no real schedule, anyway, it wasn't a big deal.

Jackie woke up and stretched her arms high above her head. She yawned and smiled sleepily. She had had wonderful dreams, about being a chef and owning a restaurant and having tons of adoring fans crowd her restaurant every night. Even though she knew it would never happen, it was nice to dream. And it didn't hurt that there was a man beside her in her dreams, though his face was blurred.

Though they weren't in a hurry, Jackie showered and dressed quickly. They had arranged to meet in the lobby for breakfast, and she didn't want to be late. She wondered what they would end up doing that day. She was leaving that in Paul's capable hands. There were a few options, based on the pamphlets and ads they had picked up at the welcome center. And after yesterday's excursions, Jackie was really up to anything. Paul had humored her. The least she could do is humor him if necessary.

He was waiting in the lobby, reading the paper in one of the plush chairs by the reception desk. He looked up and smiled when she entered the room. Jackie returned the smile.

"Sleep well?" he greeted.

"Very well. You?"

"Fine."

They were so polite. It was times like this that Jackie still felt the awkwardness that resulted from their kiss. She longed for the easy camaraderie they had developed in the beginning. But until they got back to that comfort level, she would take what she could get. "Ready for breakfast?"

"Absolutely."

They headed to the small room where a continental breakfast was served and made their selections before sitting down.

"What's on the agenda for today?" Jackie asked as she nibbled on a bagel.

"Well, it really depends on what we want to do. We could head into Mystic and check out the aquarium and the seaport, though it may be chilly to walk around. Or we could head to some outlet shops along I-95. If you're feeling historical, there are some museums and such a little farther north into the state."

Jackie shrugged. "I'm good with any of it. You pick."

"Hey, I picked yesterday."

"Hmm. Not really. The activities were dictated by what I was interested in or hadn't tried."

"True, but I pushed you into them, so it was really my idea."

"Let's agree to disagree."

"Fine. So what do we do today?"

Jackie shrugged again. "I don't know. Maybe the aquarium and seaport? We'll probably be shopping in New York tomorrow."

"Good point. Okay. Mystic it is."

Conversation over, they finished breakfast in near silence. Jackie couldn't decide if it was a comfortable silence or not. Part of her wanted to find something, anything to say, but the other part of her just wanted to sit and focus on her thoughts. Though it was hardly an argument, their little bickering was the first time they had disagreed about anything. It was unsettling, though she was sure it was bound to happen on occasion. Any two people, no matter how compatible, would disagree on occasion. She should really be grateful it wasn't worse than it had been. The entire trip had been rather amenable. She couldn't complain.

Breakfast finished, they checked out and went on their merry way. The hotel wasn't far from Mystic, so the drive wasn't long. Before they knew it they were checking out the penguins and whales, the fish and turtles and jellyfish.

It was a pleasant enough day. Jackie enjoyed the animals and the old-fashioned seaport. Despite their decision not to go shopping, they also ended up walking around Olde Mystick Village, with its quaint shops. Jackie picked up a couple of holiday gifts, then they headed back to the car.

Despite the enjoyable activities, however, the day didn't feel as comfortable as the previous one. Perhaps it was because they were both tired. Or maybe they were back to feeling awkward, strained, and the previous day had just been a break from the new norm. Whatever the reason, Jackie wasn't happy about it. And in a rare moment of courage, she decided to confront Paul about it over dinner.

She waited until they had ordered. Then, taking a sip of her water to moisten her suddenly-dry mouth, she looked up at Paul. "So what's going on with us?"

Paul nearly gagged on his own beverage. "Excuse me?"

"Don't tell me you haven't felt it."

Paul paused, looking at her with squinted eyes. "Felt what, exactly?"

"The awkwardness, the tension."

Paul leaned back in his seat. "It's still there, huh?"

"Yup."

"I'm sorry. I take full responsibility."

"It's not something to be sorry about it. I just want to know how we're going to fix it."

"Can we fix it?"

"I'd like to think so."

"Okay. What do you suggest?"

"Well..." Jackie's voice faded. This was the hardest part. "I think maybe we need to talk about things, be honest. We never really talked about...things. We glossed over them, anxious to put them behind us."

Paul sighed. "And when you say 'things' you mean the kiss, right?"

Jackie nodded, a faint blush creeping up her neck.

"Jackie, there's nothing to talk about. I'm not proud of it, but I overheard you talking to your friend Mary after it happened. I know you're not interested in a relationship with me, and for what it's worth, I agree with you. Even if there was something there, now is really not the right time to even think about pursuing it."

"So if we're on the same page, why are we still so awkward?"

"Because I'm an idiot. I still feel bad. I want to make it up to you, and I know that makes things weird, too. We haven't been as natural as we started. We've been trying too hard."

"So how do we fix it?"

Paul shrugged. "I'm open to suggestions."

"Well, if we both know we're not interested in...pursuing a relationship, then we should be fine, right? There's nothing to feel bad about. It was a lapse in judgment. As long as we don't let it happen again or do anything else to exacerbate the situation, it shouldn't be an issue."

Paul's shoulders sagged. "You're right."

"So stop feeling bad about it. I had a feeling that was why you were being so accommodating."

He shot her a half-smile. "Are you saying I was a beast before?"

She returned the smile, grateful to be on somewhat-secure footing again. "Not a beast. Just a typical guy."

"Gee thanks."

"No problem."

That settled, they attempted to have a normal dinner, filled with normal conversation. They were somewhat successful. Jackie was sure it would take time to really get that easy familiarity back, but as the meal neared its conclusion, she found she couldn't wait to get back to the hotel so she could call Mary.

As awkward as it had been, Paul was glad he and Jackie had cleared the air. He was going to have to try harder not to dwell on what had happened, and he had to stop trying so hard to make it up to her. It was over. Done. Finished. There was no reason to make a big deal out of it. It had been a single incident. There was no reason to think it would become a pattern, and therefore no reason to worry.

By the time they got back to the hotel, Paul was ready to crash. They were making an early start the next morning so they could make it to New York with plenty of time to see the sights. He had a feeling they wouldn't be spending the night in the city; he had heard it was rather expensive. But if they could at least check out a lot of what they wanted to see, they would be in decent shape. They could always stay somewhere nearby and spend a second day if they really wanted to.

He bid Jackie good night and entered his room. He tossed his coat on the chair by the TV and kicked off his shoes, then threw himself on the bed. He was exhausted. Now that he was lying down, it would be hard getting up to get changed. Maybe he would just stay as he was. He could use some sleep, and an escape from the drama. But Jackie had sure looked pretty that night, he mused as his eyes drifted shut.

Jackie was not so fortunate. She found herself wired, agitated, unable to relax. She had already planned on calling Mary, but she got ready for bed before picking up the receiver. If she was lucky, Mary would be able to calm her down enough for her to be able to rest.

"Hey, Jackie."

"Hi."

"What's the matter?"

Jackie laughed, and it felt good to release some of the tension. "You know me that well already, huh?"

Mary returned the laugh. "I guess I do. Especially since we've been communicating so much over the phone, I'm getting used to your different tones of voice. So what's up?"

Jackie sighed. "I don't know. I should be happy. We cleared the air tonight."

"Cleared the air about what?"

"You know -- the kiss."

"You're still hung up over the kiss? Uh oh. I knew it meant more."

"It doesn't. That's the thing. We both agreed that it was a mistake, a lapse in judgment, and now we're trying to get back to normal. But I still feel unsettled. I don't know why."

"Maybe because you want it to mean more."

"You've got to stop reading into things."

"I'm not reading into things. You said yourself after it first happened that you couldn't stop thinking about it. If it didn't mean anything, you should have been able to stop dwelling on it. And let me ask you this: who brought it up tonight?"

"I did, but only because I was tired of the awkwardness between us. He's been over-compensating by being super accommodating and nice. It's not natural."

"Hmm."

"What does 'hmm' mean?"

"Nothing. I'm just processing."

"Okay."

They sat in silence for a few moments until Jackie sighed again. "I'm probably making too much of this."

"It's possible. Or maybe your subconscious is trying to tell you something. Or maybe you're getting signals from him, and his subconscious is trying to tell him something."

"I'm so confused."

"Welcome to life. Aren't relationships fun?"

"We're not even *in* a relationship!"

"Hey, friendships are relationships, too. And when that line gets blurred, even just a little, it makes things a whole lot more complicated."

"I guess so." Jackie closed her eyes and leaned back on the bed. This conversation was not helping her relax. If anything she was more tense now than she had been. "So how do I uncomplicate it?"

"It'll just take time. If you truly don't have feelings for each other, the awkwardness will pass. Just try to enjoy the trip and don't dwell on that one incident."

"That's kind of what we decided tonight. But it's easier said than done."

"I know. Your mind starts going in a million different directions, and the more you try not to think about it, the more you think about it."

"Exactly."

"It'll get easier. Just do things to get your mind off it. What's on the agenda for tomorrow?"

"We're going to New York City."

"Well, that'll get your mind off things. What do you have planned?"

"Not quite sure yet. Paul had a bunch of stuff he printed off the internet. We usually swing by the states' welcome centers, but since we're just hitting the corner of the state, we probably won't see a welcome center before we hit the city. So we'll have to go off the research he did."

"Good luck. I hear driving in New York is a nightmare."

"Thanks for the vote of confidence."

"No problem. You just might want to think about stopping somewhere and taking a train in or something."

"That's something to think about. I'll have to discuss it with Paul. He's the one who'll be driving."

"Okay."

"So what's new on your end?"

"Oh, same old, same old. Though the morning sickness seems to be easing up a bit. I'm very grateful for that. I can actually keep my breakfast down most mornings now."

"That's a good thing."

"Definitely. I must say, though, with my not feeling well, Bryan has definitely been picking up the slack. He's been spoiling me. It's going to be hard to get back into the swing of things once I'm up and running again."

"I'm glad he's been treating you well. You deserve it."

"Thanks. I really can't complain. For a spur-of-the-moment decision, this marriage was probably the best thing to ever happen to me."

Jackie smiled to herself, but it was a sad smile. She longed to have that kind of comfort with someone, to be content and secure in a relationship with someone. That was definitely something she was going to have to work on when she got back home. She had to add that to her list of things to change: find a man! But not just any man. He had to be kind, and intelligent and funny. Not stand-up-com-ic kind of funny, just enough to make her laugh when she was upset and cheer her up when she was down. She wasn't too picky, but he had to be a good man, not a jerk. Was that asking too much?

"...and we had Melanie and Bobby over for dinner. I can't believe how much little Cameron has grown."

Jackie had missed a lot of what Mary was saying, but her mind was moving on before she could even feel bad. Children would be nice, too, though she wasn't getting any younger. She wasn't opposed to adopting, though, if she couldn't have kids herself. By the time she met someone and got married, she would probably be too old to have a child safely. At least for her own peace of mind. But there were plenty of children out there who needed loving homes. She wouldn't mind opening her heart to one or two of them. Or even more...she loved kids.

"When you get back, you should come over for dinner, too."

"Sure. That sounds good." Fortunately Mary didn't seem to notice that Jackie had disappeared there for a bit. "Or maybe I could have you over for dinner."

"Really?"

"Yeah." Her heart started beating more quickly. The invitation was out there now.

"I didn't know you cooked."

"Well, I do. Just for myself. But I'm thinking of taking some courses, maybe try something new."

"That's great!"

"Thanks. The classes won't start until December, so I have some time. But I'm thinking they'll get my feet wet and see if it's something I want to do."

"Want to do? Like in a career?"

"Maybe."

"Wow. I had no idea."

"Yeah. Me neither." Jackie gave a nervous laugh. "And nothing may come of it. I still don't know if I would feel comfortable cooking for other people. But Paul suggested I start small, maybe just have a person or two over for dinner and try it out. So..."

"I think it's a great idea. And I'll support you in any way I can. Once I can keep things down for good, I'd be more than happy to try out anything you want to dish up." Mary laughed.

"Sounds like a plan." Jackie laughed, too, then sighed. "Well, I should probably get going. We plan on making an early start of things."

"Okay. I'm getting sleepy myself. I'll catch you in a couple of days?"

"Of course."

"Great. Have fun in New York."

"We will."

They said their good-byes, and Jackie replaced the receiver. What a whirlwind of a conversation. Though they hadn't really settled anything with regards to Jackie's awkward relationship with Paul, Jackie felt a little better. She would just bide her time and hope things got more comfortable. And it wasn't as if she didn't have anything else to think about, especially with all these changes she was determined to make. A husband, and children and career change, oh my!

Chapter 14

Paul woke up just before his alarm, a smile on his face. The smile quickly faded, though, when he realized the cause of the smile: he had dreamed about Jackie. Especially after their discussion last night, that was the last thing that he should be doing. Not that he had any say in the matter. But he could faintly remember thinking about her as he drifted off to sleep. He really had to stop doing that. They could never get back onto even footing if he let his mind play tricks on him. That was simply not acceptable.

Getting up, he opted for a cold shower to wake him up and hopefully knock some sense into him. He had to be natural, relaxed, when he met Jackie for breakfast. He couldn't let her know what was running through his mind. And the best way to do that was deny those thoughts were there to begin with.

Paul started running through old medical research he had done in college -- anything to get his mind off his companion. Maybe he should think about his impending divorce. That should clear things up right away. How could he even be thinking about another woman when he was still legally married? When just a couple of weeks ago he was contemplating doing everything in his power to hold on to his marriage? What was wrong with him?

Thinking about Pam was a definite wake-up call, and he was able to get himself presentable without thinking about his dreams again. Now he just had to get through the day, and he should be fine. By tomorrow the memories should have faded.

He was the first one down as usual, though Jackie wasn't far behind. He had barely opened the newspaper when she arrived in the lobby. She smiled at him, and, though it was a tentative smile, he could tell she was trying. He smiled back and folded the paper.

Breakfast wasn't quite awkward; rather it felt more like the first couple of meals they had shared: shy and polite. Not perfect, but it gave him hope that they could return to where they were. As long as he didn't let his mind wander too much. The key would be keeping his mind occupied. And today that shouldn't be a problem. New York was filled with things to do, and while they hadn't finalized their plans, he knew they had several items they wanted to check out. Playing tourist should kill several hours and keep his mind occupied. He could hope anyway.

To Jackie it seemed like Paul was still faking something, but she couldn't fault him for at least trying. They were both trying. And it would take time, as Mary had said, for them to get back to where they had been. She was sure today would be good for them.

New York flew by. They opted to park outside of the city and take the train in, so they felt like true New Yorkers taking the subway around Manhattan. The day was filled with hot tourist spots like the Statue of Liberty and Ellis Island, and a bit of shopping and people-watching in Times Square. They decided on a low-key dinner so they could splurge on tickets to an up-and-coming Broadway show, and Jackie couldn't have been happier. She had always loved the theater, and it had been a dream to see something on Broadway. The intimate theater wasn't quite what she expected, but she certainly couldn't complain about the view. The play was terrific, and by the time they headed back to their car, she was content. It had been a great day, filled with new experiences, and Jackie was satisfied that she had seen some of New York's best. But she was exhausted!

Paul bid Jackie good-night and headed to his room, eyes drooping. They had decided to get a bit of a later start the next morning since they had had such a busy day, followed by a late night. He wasn't complaining though; the day had been as close to ideal as he could hope for. He saw sights he had always wanted to see, and spending the time with Jackie had made the activities even more enjoyable. Too enjoyable, probably.

Despite his reassurances to the contrary, Paul was afraid he was starting to fall for her. The thought alarmed him. Surely he couldn't be serious. It had to just be a passing fling. Perhaps being in such close proximity to her for extended periods of time was just making her more comfortable, more appealing, to him. How else could he explain it? He was hardly over Pam, for crying out loud! He certainly couldn't just jump into another relationship. The feelings had to be superficial at best.

Yet, he couldn't help comparing her to Pam. They were completely different. Pam was driven, stubborn, focused. She had her priorities and had no problem knocking down anyone that stood in the way of those priorities. Jackie, on the other hand, was pensive, considerate. While no less competent than Pam, she had a more genuine, caring way of getting things done that appealed to Paul.

Maybe that was what had driven him and Pam apart. Maybe they were too different. He had certainly been drawn to her charisma, her confidence, in college. But he was a doctor; he cared about people. While Pam wasn't exactly heartless, she also wasn't warm and fuzzy. Her bedside manner would have left many patients cold, while Paul was known for his kind, upbeat nature. He had always thought they balanced each other, and that their differences had been part of the appeal. Opposites attract, after all. But perhaps they had been too different. Maybe that's why Pam hadn't been happy with him. Maybe Pam wanted hm to be more like her, and he wanted her to be more like him. While Jackie...well, Jackie was exactly what he would describe his ideal companion to be. Attractive, yes, but she wasn't drop-dead gorgeous. Pam would likely win when it came to outward appearances. But Jackie's kind-hearted nature made her appealing to the eye. Her eyes were warm, softening even more when she worked with children. She was competent, capable, but she didn't dwell on her abilities; they were simply part of who she was. She was confident in her job. She thought things through, was careful in her actions and her words, yet wasn't afraid to acknowledge her weak points. Even if she was afraid of the changes she talked about making, she wasn't afraid to tackle them. Her self-control was remarkable.

Paul thought about all this as he got ready for bed. By the time he rested his head on the pillow, he had all but convinced himself that the "superficial" feelings he had started to feel weren't superficial after all. Could he seriously be falling for Jackie? She would never go along with it, of that he was sure. Their conversation, and the conversation he had overheard between her and her friend Mary, told him that he didn't stand a chance, even if he wanted to take things further. Which meant only one thing: he had to talk himself out of this. He had to think about ways in which Jackie was lacking.

By the time Paul's eyes drifted shut, he still hadn't thought of a single one.

Chapter 15

Jackie sensed a change in Paul the following morning, but she tried not to dwell on it. They were both tired, and with a relatively quiet day ahead of them, she was sure they were both concerned that the awkwardness would return. But she was determined not to let it affect things. She was going to put on a smile and make the best of the situation. It was all she could do.

They met in the lobby as per their usual, then proceeded to breakfast. Conversation was limited, and they ate quickly, then retrieved their suitcases and checked out.

Paul was still quiet when they got into the car and began driving away, but Jackie was afraid to ask him about it. She had already brought up the awkward conversations before, and she didn't want to come across as a nag. So she settled in to her seat and pulled out the paperwork Paul had printed about New Jersey.

When they stopped for lunch, Jackie couldn't help herself. "Are you okay?" It was a simple question that she hoped would at least get them back on more comfortable footing.

Paul sighed and nodded his head, then seemed to change his mind and shook his head instead. "I don't want to burden you. I'll be fine."

Jackie leaned back in the plastic chair and assessed him. "You think sitting there, silent and sulking, is any better?"

Paul grinned. "You're getting more outspoken. I like that."

Jackie blushed.

Paul's grin faded. "I like you, Jackie."

"You're not so bad yourself."

"No, I mean I like you. Last night I realized that maybe that kiss wasn't so accidental. Maybe my subconscious just knew before I could admit it to myself."

Jackie could only stare wide-eyed at the man sitting across from her. "Paul, I --"

He held up a hand. "I know. We're not doing anything about it. You don't have feelings for me, and even if you did, the timing is not right. I know. I get it. That's why I've been so quiet. I didn't want to make things awkward again."

"I'm sorry, Paul."

"It's nothing to feel sorry about. You didn't do anything wrong."

Jackie didn't know how to respond, but Paul started eating, so she did, too. So much for hoping things would get back to comfortable. She had never been in a position like this before.

They were about halfway through their meal, each lost in thought, when a chirping startled Jackie out of her musings. "Is that your phone?"

"Yeah. I wonder who would be calling me." He slipped the phone out of its case at his waist and looked at the screen. "It's my mom." Brows furrowed, he answered the call.

Jackie watched him as she continued eating. It didn't take long for his face to get pale and a mixture of emotions she had never seen fill his eyes. "Everything okay?"

Paul could only shake his head as he listened to his mother. "Okay. I'll be there as soon as I can. I'm in New Jersey right now." A couple of "uh-huhs" and then he hung up the phone.

He was silent for a moment, and Jackie couldn't help but ask "what happened?"

"Uncle Bill's in the hospital. Heart attack. It doesn't look good."

"Oh my God."

"I'm sorry, Jackie, but I think our trip is going to have to get cut short."

"That's not a problem. Let me just run to the ladies' room and we can go."

Paul nodded, and she scurried off. She needed a moment to compose herself. What a crazy day it had turned out to be. Silence, followed by a confession she definitely hadn't been expecting, and now this. She could only hope that Dr. Collins would be all right.

Jackie considered calling Mary to let her know that the trip was over, but that conversation would be too long, all things considered. It would just have to wait until they got home.

⁓ ℓℓ ⁓

Paul was pacing by the front door when Jackie returned from the restroom. He ran a hand through his hair, nodded once, and proceeded out the door in silence. He should have known something was wrong as soon as he saw it was his mom calling. She never called him. But he naively thought that perhaps she was calling about the holidays, though it was still a bit early. The last thing he expected was to get the news about Uncle Bill. Maybe that was why he was taking it so hard. No, he would have been a mess even if he had suspected. With all the time they'd been spending together lately, he and Bill had gotten close. The old man was more of a father to him than his real father was. What would he do without him?

The drive was much too long, despite Paul driving faster than he ever had in his life. He could only be grateful that they hadn't gotten farther south. The few hours spent in the car now were much better than the day spent in the car if they were driving back from Florida or some other such place.

With nothing more than brief words and phrases, they agreed to head right to the hospital. Bill was Jackie's boss, so she had just as much concern for him as Paul did. Yet the only evidence of her fears was the wringing of her hands in her lap. Paul envied her outward strength and composure. He knew he looked less than put-together, with tousled hair and a possessed look in his eye. He prayed that he didn't get pulled over. One look at him and any cop would thing he was drunk or worse.

But luck was with him, and as they pulled into the hospital parking lot he squeezed Jackie's hands just before putting the car in park.

"Thanks, Jackie."

"For what?" She turned to look at him.

"For being here. And being a pillar of strength."

"I don't feel very strong."

"Maybe not, but you look it." He attempted a smile. "I'm just glad I don't have to head up there alone."

Jackie nodded and closed her eyes. A moment later they were walking through the front door.

Paul's mother and stepfather were sitting in a bench outside Bill's door. His mother looked drawn, exhausted. Wordlessly she stood up and enveloped Paul in a tight embrace. Paul could hear her sobs against his shoulder, and he held her tight for several moments. It couldn't be easy seeing your older brother so close to the end. Paul swallowed. It wouldn't be easy for him, either.

His stepfather was less demonstrative with his emotions, but the grip of his handshake told Paul he was no less affected. It would be a long night for all of them.

Paul introduced his parents to Jackie before they entered Bill's room. Paul ignored the questioning looks in their eyes and led Jackie into the room by hand. There would be plenty of time for explanations later, though he wasn't looking forward to it.

Bill was pale, weak. Paul couldn't remember him ever having looked as helpless. Yet Bill still managed to smile ever so slightly when he opened his eyes and saw them approach. Bill tried to lift one hand in greeting, but it barely made it off the bed.

"Paul." The voice was raspy. "Jackie. What are you doing here?"

Paul pulled up a chair beside his uncle. "What do you think we're doing here? We came to see you. Mom called."

"Silly woman. She always worries over nothing."

"I don't think it's nothing this time, Uncle Bill."

Bill coughed. "I know." He turned to Jackie. "How was the trip?"

Jackie attempted a smile. "Interesting."

"You'll have to tell me all about it."

"When you're feeling up to it."

Jackie pulled up another chair, and they all sat in silence until a coughing fit shook Bill's body.

Bill sighed and leaned his head back on the bed. "I'm afraid this might be the end."

"Don't talk like that." Paul reached forward and grabbed one of his uncle's hands. "You're the strongest person I know. You'll get through it."

Bill turned slightly toward Paul. "You're a good boy. But you're wrong. I've known for a while that the end was near. Why do you think I was so anxious to retire? I didn't want to leave my patients without care. I know you'll take good care of them, just like you're meant to. And Jackie will help you."

Jackie looked away, and Paul could see a blush creeping up her neck. "Jackie won't be joining me. She's decided to pursue other endeavors."

The shock seemed to give Bill a moment of strength. "That can't be true. Jackie?"

Jackie turned back toward them and nodded. "I'm sorry, Dr. Collins. After the trip and everything, I thought it would be best for Paul and me to part ways. But I'll make sure he has someone even better to help him."

"There is no one better. You ran that office like a well-oiled machine."

Paul looked down at his hands. After everything that had happened, he couldn't blame Jackie for moving on. Apparently she was even smarter than he thought, realizing the awkwardness the trip was likely to cause before he even considered it. And now...well, she probably wouldn't have come to work for him even if she hadn't decided it before they departed. He certainly wouldn't blame her. But he would miss her.

Bill closed his eyes. "I'm sorry to hear it. But I wish you the best of luck."

"Thank you." Jackie's voice was barely audible.

"So tell me about this trip. Did you find what you were looking for?"

Paul cleared his throat. "We started in Maine, but we only got as far as Jersey. I guess the rest of the trip will have to wait."

"Maybe that was all the trip you needed."

"Maybe. But it would be nice to see the southern states one of these days."

"You will."

"Someday."

"So did you find what you were looking for?" Bill repeated.

Paul leaned back and thought for a moment. What had he even been looking for? Clarity? Freedom? The open road had been nice, and he had had hope that it would clear his mind. But getting hung up on Jackie had certainly affected things.

Then again, there had been that time last night he had spent thinking about Pam. It was probably the first time he had ever really thought about her so objectively. And it had made him more at peace with the divorce, even if it had complicated matters between him and Jackie. "Somewhat," he answered.

Bill nodded his head slightly. "Good. And you, Jackie? Was it everything you had hoped for?"

For once Jackie looked unsettled. Paul had never seen her squirm before. "I don't know what I was hoping for. But it definitely shook things up a bit."

Bill smiled. "Good. You could use a little shaking up."

"I suppose I could." She attempted a smile.

Moments later Bill's eyes drifted shut, and his breathing became heavy. Jackie turned to Paul. "I should probably go. This is a time for family."

Paul looked up at her. He saw the sorrow in her eyes, and he felt a twinge in his belly. "I'll take you home."

"It's okay. I'll call Mary or something. You should stay."

He could only nod in agreement. He didn't really want to leave Bill's side, though he felt bad about abandoning her. "I'm sorry."

"There's nothing to be sorry about." She patted his hand.

"Can I call you tomorrow?"

"Of course. And if anything...happens, call me, too."

"I will."

He walked her out of the room and bid her farewell in the hallway just outside. His parents were no longer occupying the bench in the hall, and he was grateful. He didn't want to talk about Pam or Jackie or the upheaval his life was going through. He just wanted to focus on Uncle Bill and what little time they had left together.

Jackie waited until she was in the lobby before she pulled out her cell phone. She hoped Mary was home; there was certainly plenty to talk about, even if she couldn't get a ride home.

Mary picked up after two rings. "Hello?"

"Hey, Mary."

"Jackie! You're calling early. Everything all right?"

Jackie sighed. "Well, not exactly. I'm back. Well, not back exactly. I'm at Rockford Memorial. Any chance I can get a ride?"

"Rockford! What on earth are you doing at the hospital? Are you okay?"

"I'm fine. It's really kind of a long story."

"Okay. We can talk in the car. I'll be there in twenty minutes."

Jackie collapsed into a chair in the lobby while she waited. What a day. Even if it hadn't been an emotional roller coaster before, Dr. Collins's question had thrown her off. Was the trip everything she had hoped for?

Despite cutting the trip short, she definitely felt different. It was hard to believe that less than two weeks ago she was terrified to leave her little house and embark on an adventure. But now? Now she couldn't say that she hadn't done anything out of the ordinary. She had seen places she had never seen, tasted things she had never tasted, experienced things she had never experienced. And it had all changed her. Perhaps in little ways, but she was different now. She didn't feel as timid, as shy as she had been. Maybe she hadn't undergone some earth-shattering life changes, but her perspective had changed. She guessed that's what living without plans and experiencing new things did for you.

The real question now was: what was she going to do about it? So she had lived this somewhat-grand adventure. What would she do with the knowledge she had gained?

Mary entered the lobby, interrupting Jackie's musings. Jackie greeted her with a smile, despite a churning stomach. Mary cocked her head to one side and studied her.

"I thought you were supposed to find yourself and all that. You look more confused now than when you left."

"Let's just say it's been an eventful day."

"Well, tell me all about it. Ready to go?"

Jackie nodded and followed Mary to the parking garage. Once they were settled, Mary put the car in reverse and ordered Jackie to "spill it."

Jackie didn't know where to start. Mary knew pretty much everything up to the events of the day. Perhaps it would be easiest to start with the previous evening.

"Well, yesterday we were in New York, as you know. It was a great day, actually. We saw lots of things, played tourist for a bit, did a little shopping. All in all it was a nice day. Paul and I were getting along, and it seemed like we were getting back to a comfortable place."

"But?"

"This morning he was weird. There's no other word for it. He could barely look me in the eye, he hardly said a word, and he was just strange. We went on our way, but by lunch I was tired of it. So I asked him if everything was okay."

When it came down to it, Jackie could still hardly believe what Paul had confessed. It was too foreign a concept to her. She had had relationships before, but it wasn't often a man had announced his feelings to her without prompting or encouragement.

"So what did he say?"

Jackie took a deep breath. "First, he tried to brush it off. But I wasn't having any of that. Eventually he spit it out."

"And?" Mary glanced at Jackie. "What was it?"

"Basically, he admitted he had feelings for me." There, she had said it. It was awkward, and she still didn't know how it made her feel, but it was out there.

"Wow. So here I was thinking the kiss meant something on your end, but it was really something on his end."

"I guess so. Though I don't think he really knew it at the time."

"So what did you say?"

"Not much. I didn't have to say anything. Even before I could respond he acknowledged that it wasn't the right time, even if I did feel the same way, and that he knew there wasn't anything we could do about it."

"So how did you end up at the hospital? Did you decide to come home after that?"

"We hadn't made any decisions. While we were eating lunch, Paul's mother called. His uncle had a heart attack and was in the hospital."

"His uncle -- your boss?"

Jackie nodded. "Yup."

"Wow. How's he doing?"

Jackie sighed and closed her eyes. "Not good. He seems to think it's the end. Based on how he looked and his defeatist attitude, I think he's right. But I'll be sorry to see him go. He's a great man."

They rode in silence for a few minutes. Tears had started to well in Jackie's eyes, and she sniffled quietly. She really would miss Dr. Collins. Over the past ten years he had become more than a boss; he was a friend, a mentor. While Jackie wasn't one to open up to others very often, she knew she could always go to him if there was something troubling her. And he had been a fair boss, treating his employees with respect and consideration.

Of course thinking about that made her think about everything else: what she was going to do with her life, how she was going to make it through even a few weeks with Paul as her boss, and how the office would change. She wondered if anyone had notified his patients, or other employees. Perhaps she should take care of that when she got home. She was technically still employed in that office, and it would be easy to slip back into her role. Efficient, responsible Jackie -- that was her. And a couple of weeks of freedom hadn't changed her that much.

Paul was torn between watching Uncle Bill sleep and waiting in the hallway. He wasn't much use either way, but he didn't want to leave. What if something happened? He would never forgive himself. Seeing his parents approach down the hallway answered his question for him. Wanting to avoid their questions as long as possible, he slipped back into the room and sat in the chair by Bill's bed.

He didn't know how long he had been sitting there when Bill opened his eyes. After a moment of haziness, Bill turned to look at Paul. A tiny smile tugged at the corners of his mouth.

"You're still here."

"Of course I am. Where else would I be?"

Bill turned his head back to look at the ceiling. "Jackie left?"

"Yeah."

"What happened on your trip?"

"What do you mean?"

"She seemed uncomfortable. She's never like that. Jackie is the epitome of poise."

"I'm afraid I went and did something stupid."

"You fell for her, didn't you?"

Paul looked up at his uncle. "Is it that obvious?"

"Maybe not, but I had a feeling it would happen."

"Why didn't you talk me out of asking her to come then?"

"Because I knew she would be good for you. She's a much better match for you than that woman you're married to."

Paul sighed. "I was kind of thinking the same thing myself. But I still love Pam. How messed up is that?"

"Love is always messed up. Even in a relationship as seemingly simple as mine and your aunt's, things get complicated."

"So what do I do?"

Bill attempted a shrug. "Well, even if you two are meant to be together, which I can't say if you are or not, now is not the time."

Paul ran his fingers through his hair. "I know."

"You have to get your divorce finalized first. It wouldn't be fair to string Jackie along through that. Of course, that's assuming she even feels the same way. Does she?"

"I don't think so."

"Hmm."

"I know. It's a mess. But I've got to put it behind me. Now that we're not confined in a car together, maybe it'll be easier to get past this."

"Perhaps."

They sat in silence for a few moments. Paul thought perhaps Bill had fallen asleep again. It startled him when Bill started to talk again.

"I know you probably don't want to talk about this, but it has to be done."

"No, it doesn't."

"Yes, it does. I've made you the executor of my estate. It shouldn't be too difficult; most of it I've left to you."

"Me? Why me? Why not Mom?"

Bill sighed. "Your mother will get some things, but she wouldn't appreciate everything like you would. You get the house, for example. I know how much you like it. And you'll need a place to live."

"I --" Paul didn't know what to say. He didn't want to think about his uncle dying or being in that big, empty house without him.

"I love you, Paul. You're the closest thing I have to a son. I know you'll make me proud, with the practice and with life. You'll figure it out. You were always a smart cookie. No reason that should change now."

Tears were pricking Paul's eyes. Why did it feel like his uncle was saying good-bye?"

"It's time, Paul. I'm okay with it. I want you to know that. Tell your mother I love her, too."

A moment later the tears were running down Paul's cheeks as Bill slipped away.

Chapter 16

It had been three days, and Paul still expected Bill to greet him when he got home. The house was even bigger and emptier than he had expected, and when he stepped over the threshold after the funeral, the wave of sadness swept over him, bringing tears to his eyes once again. He wondered if he would ever get used to it.

Jackie had been at the funeral, of course, but their conversation had been limited to words of sorrow and a brief discussion of work. Being ever-efficient, Jackie had notified all the employees and patients of what had happened, and rescheduled all appointments for the rest of the week. While Paul wasn't looking forward to returning to the office, he knew he couldn't let his patients down. And that's what they were -- his patients. The signed documents had been waiting for him at the lawyer's office. The practice was now his. The house, many of its contents, and the car were all his, too, or they would be once probate was completed. He didn't look forward to the process, but as executor he had no choice. And, if nothing else, Uncle Bill had asked it of him. That was enough for him.

Paul hung his coat up in the front closet and went to the kitchen to pour himself a drink. He had no idea how he would fill the empty hours ahead of him. TV should numb his pain for a couple of hours. Maybe he would fall asleep on the couch as had become his norm.

He was just lifting the glass to his lips when the doorbell rang. Putting the glass down, he went to answer it.

Pam was waiting on the doorstep. Though surprised, he invited her in.

They had exchanged polite words, civil words, at the funeral. She stood by his side, offering strength and comfort, though he was too numb to notice much. He hadn't even told his parents they were getting divorced yet. There had been too much else to think about, to worry about. In retrospect, perhaps the change in topic would have been a welcome reprieve.

And now, here she was. What was she doing there?

Perhaps she didn't have a reason, because three hours later they were still just chatting. Sitting with her, talking about anything and everything, Paul realized what had drawn him to her in the first place: she was opinionated, strong-willed, but willing to see things from all sides. While he couldn't help but compare her to Jackie, it was nice knowing that Pam wasn't the horrible person he had been tempted to believe she was the other night. Perhaps there was hope that they could at least be friends after all was said and done.

"Not that I don't appreciate you stopping by or anything, but just out of curiosity, why did you come here?"

Pam sighed and looked at the wine glass in her hand. "I don't know. I guess I just knew that you were taking this hard, and I wanted to be there for you. It can't be easy living in this house all alone after everything."

"It's not. I appreciate the company. It just surprised me, is all."

"It surprised me, too. I didn't expect to come over. But when I left the funeral I realized I didn't have anywhere specific to be this afternoon, and I figured you didn't, either. And maybe you wouldn't want to be alone."

"Thank you, Pam. I mean that. It's nice to know we can still be civil after everything. I hope we can still be friends."

"I'd like that." She smiled at him.

They sat in silence for a moment before Pam uncrossed her legs and stood up. "I should probably get going."

"Okay."

"I have an hour drive ahead of me, and I don't want to catch traffic."

"Not a problem."

Paul walked Pam to the door and helped her with her coat. As he opened the door for her, she turned toward him.

"It was great seeing you, Paul."

"You, too." He leaned in to kiss her cheek, but Pam turned her face so their lips met. After a moment Paul pulled away. "I'm sorry, Pam. We can't."

Pam sighed. "I know. Have a good night."

He watched her go somewhat wistfully. A couple of weeks ago he would have jumped at the opportunity to kiss her, to be with her. Now he just felt hollow and empty inside. It had been nice to see her, to talk with her, but the instant she was gone, he was back to being alone -- and confused. He could use his uncle's guidance. But that was no longer an option.

Sighing, Paul closed the door and returned to the family room where he picked up the wine glasses to bring to the kitchen. Cleaning them filled a couple of minutes, but he knew it wouldn't be long before he was zoning out to the TV. At least being with Pam had helped the time pass. And it really had been nice to talk to her, to feel a connection that had been lacking between them for quite some time now. Perhaps they would be better as friends, without the tension and expectations of a relationship straining things.

He wandered around the house a bit before ending up in the family room once again. Within minutes he had turned on the TV and settled himself on the sofa. It would be another long night. He wondered what Jackie was doing...

Jackie was staring out the window, nursing a cup of tea. The day's events had hit her hard, as she had known they would. Dr. Collins had been her boss for ten years. He had been seemingly healthy, vibrant and occasionally boisterous. True, he was a little overweight and had a fondness for cigars, but nothing horribly unhealthy. It was hard to think of him as being gone.

A light snow had started to fall, reminding Jackie of the storm that had trapped her and Paul in Boston. It seemed years ago now, but it had been barely a week. She hadn't been lying when she had told Dr. Collins that the trip had shaken her up. And now that the trip was over, she had some decisions to make. She would only be able to work with Paul for so long. The awkwardness was sure to linger, and she had already told him she wasn't coming back permanently. The temp they had hired to cover for Jackie while she was away had worked out well, and they were likely going to offer her the position. That gave Jackie even less time, since there would be considerably less training required.

So what was she going to do? The trip was supposed to inspire her, not only to make changes in her life, but to figure out what she wanted to do. The only thing that had ignited her passion was the food expo that they had attended. She had known before that she liked to cook, and she had already decided to take a class or two. But she was nowhere near qualified to take it on as a career. No one would hire her without a degree from a cooking school. So what should she do? Start at the bottom, in a job that didn't require the degree, then work her way up when she got one? Did she even want to go to cooking school? And what would she do until then? Wash dishes? Be a waitress? Work at McDonalds?

Jackie turned from the window and collapsed into a dining chair. Okay, so she was starting to lose her fear of making changes. But the one good thing that had been present when she didn't change was knowing where she was heading. Every day she would wake up and know what that day would bring. Some variations, of course, but for the most part she knew what to expect. She excelled at her job, so every year she got a glowing review, followed by a modest raise. Her bills were paid on time, her retirement savings was growing, and she had enough money in the bank to cover her if anything unforeseen were to happen.

And now? Now she had no idea what tomorrow would bring. For all she knew, Paul would say the new receptionist was working out great, and they no longer needed Jackie. Jackie could be out on the street with no notice. While she didn't think Paul would do that to her, she really had no way of knowing for sure. And she would have no one to blame but herself. While, all things considered, she had probably made the right choice, she couldn't help but wonder if she would be happier right now if she hadn't said she would leave.

With a deep breath, Jackie fortified herself. She had to stop letting fear control her. It was time to look at things rationally. Tomorrow she would start looking for a job. She would scroll the online job boards, flip through the newspaper and try to find something that would interest her. She wouldn't look for receptionist or office positions – those would be her back-up if she couldn't find something that sparked her interest more. In the meantime, she would take a good hard look at her finances and figure out how long she could last without a job. Without looking at the numbers, she was fairly certain she had enough to last several months at least. She wasn't one to spend frivolously, so any income brought in, after normal expenses and her occasional splurge, went right into savings. The impromptu road trip had eaten into it a bit, but considering they had cut the trip short, it hadn't made much of a dent.

Of course if she decided to take classes or go to cooking school, that would cost money, too. And she had no idea how much those would cost. But she would love to take some classes. She had always loved learning, and perhaps they would help her decide what she wanted to do. But if she couldn't afford classes until she got a job, then what would she do for a job? Would it just be a shot in the dark, hoping it worked out?

Jackie put down her mug and rubbed her temples. There were too many decisions to make, and she was ill-equipped to make them. She felt as if she didn't know who she was, what she wanted. Perhaps what she really needed was some time on her own, to reflect on her life without the drama of a road trip companion clouding her thoughts. What had started as a journey of self-discovery had turned into a dramatic exploration of a relationship – or lack thereof. Too much time and energy had been spent dwelling over what was or was not happening between her and Paul. And that was not what she needed right now. Perhaps a walk would help clear her head.

Chapter 17

The air was brisk, and the crispness of it cleared Paul's head. Gentle snowflakes settled around him, falling on his eyelashes until his vision blurred. Closing his eyes, he took a deep breath. This was what he needed. He needed a cold winter day to get his mind off the drama and decisions that had clouded him since Pam had said she wanted a divorce. He needed to step away from it all, stop thinking about Pam and Uncle Bill and Jackie and the practice that had fallen into his lap much sooner than anticipated.

Paul took a step off the porch and began to wander down the street. He didn't have a destination in mind, but it was nice to get out of the house. There were too many memories stifling him there. Taking a walk would help. Maybe then he could feel at peace.

The world was quiet. The occasional car passed, but otherwise he was alone with the night. He could see houses with lit windows, but they seemed so far away, little sanctuaries beyond his reach. The people he could see within were foreign, strangers, little wisps of his imagination.

He was just thinking about turning around when he spotted another bundled-up figure heading in his direction. With its head down, it was difficult to make out any features, yet something about the shape was familiar. Paul paused to allow the figure to get closer.

"Jackie?" His voice was raspy from the cold and disuse.

She looked up, startled. It took a moment for her eyes to clear. She had obviously been deep in thought. It was likely her mind had been as clouded as his had been, filled with the decisions she had to make and the chaos of the past few weeks. What was going through that head of hers?

"Paul?" She blinked rapidly and cocked her head to one side.

"Hi."

"I didn't expect to see you. Do you live close by?"

Paul gestured to his left. "Down that way a few streets. I've been walking a bit. How are you?"

Jackie shrugged. "All right, I guess. A little shaken up."

"Yeah. Me, too."

They stood in silence for a few moments until Paul saw Jackie shake. "You're shivering."

Jackie shrugged again. "It's winter. It's cold outside." She attempted a smile.

"Do you live far?"

"No."

"That's good."

It was awkward being with her. He didn't know what to say, what to do. Part of him was drawn to her, and part of him wanted to slap himself for everything that had transpired between them.

"Do you want to maybe grab a cup of coffee?"

"Where?"

Paul looked around. They were in the middle of a residential area. There wouldn't be a café for miles. He sighed. "I don't know. It just seemed like the thing to do. I feel like we need to talk."

"I don't know if that's a good idea."

"Why not?"

"I think maybe it would be better if we just went our separate ways, let whatever happened lie."

"I –" Paul didn't know what to say. He knew there was a good chance that Jackie didn't share whatever it was he felt, but he hadn't expected to have to break off all contact with her. And pretend as if nothing had happened at all. "What about work?"

"I will, of course, return for as long as necessary until you find a replacement. But I don't expect it to take very long. It's my understanding the temp worked out rather well."

"We'll have to talk at work."

"I can remain a professional if you can."

Paul shoved his hands in his pockets. "Of course I can be a professional. I just..."

"We're both confused, Paul. We both have decisions to make, changes to make. I'm sorry, but worrying about you can't be on my list of things to do. I have enough to worry about."

Silence fell.

"I'm sorry if that sounded mean."

Paul closed his eyes and took a deep breath. "It wasn't mean. I don't think you have a mean bone in your body." He gave her a half-smile. "I know you're right. I guess I just figured that after all we've been through, we're kind of connected now. I didn't think I'd have to give you up so soon."

Jackie turned away. "I think maybe that's part of the problem." Her voice was quiet, soft. But she took in a deep breath and looked back up at him. "What happened between us – it can't happen, Paul. Not now, maybe not ever. Even if I was interested, I refuse to be a rebound for you. And that's all I could be. You have things to figure out with your wife. For Pete's sake, the divorce papers probably haven't even been filed. And while we did share a very memorable experience with our road trip, it will always be tainted with that knowledge. I think a clean split will be best."

"I'm sorry, Jackie."

"It's nothing to be sorry about."

"Of course it is. You said it yourself. Our road trip was supposed to help you figure things out, and now it will always be tainted because I went and did something stupid. I had hoped we could move past it, that I could make it up to you in some way, but I know you're probably right. A clean split is probably best." He sighed. "I just don't know how I'm going to make it through without you. Which is strange, considering a month ago I didn't even know you existed."

"Funny how things can change so quickly, huh?"

Paul didn't feel like laughing. He felt like curling up in bed and never getting up. First Pam, then Uncle Bill and now Jackie. It was starting to look like he was destined to be alone. And it felt like someone had punched him in the gut.

"So I guess that's it?"

Jackie nodded. "I'm sorry, Paul."

"Like you said, it's nothing to be sorry about. I wish things could be different, but I know you're right."

Silence fell again, and Paul watched his foot brush at the snow on the pavement. The peacefulness of the evening had been swept away, only to be replaced by an overwhelming sadness.

"So I'll see you Monday?"

Paul nodded. It was all he could manage at the moment.

"Okay."

She stayed for a moment, as if she wanted to say something else, but a minute later she was walking away. Paul lifted his head to watch her go before turning around and heading back home.

Chapter 18

Jackie barely made it home before the tears began slipping from her eyes. She had been in no condition to meet Paul, and yet it was done. Over. Now she knew where she stood. She was surprised she had been able to be so firm, so confident. At least now she could say one decision was made. Paul would be out of her life. The thought made her slightly uneasy, though she knew it was for the best.

She also knew that she still had a job. That helped a little, but she didn't know how long she could rely on that. She had been firm on that point as well. She only wished that some of the confidence and determination she had displayed would carry over into the rest of her life. The walk had done nothing to ease her mind on the rest of the decisions that had to be made.

Jackie tossed her keys on the table by the door and hung up her coat and scarf in the closet. She stood for a moment, looking at the row of garments on their hangers, neat and ready for her at a moment's notice. She was tempted to grab them all and throw them to the floor. It wasn't fair that they should look so put-together when she was feeling anything but. Resisting the urge, Jackie instead slid to the floor and burst into tears. How had things gotten so messed up? True, she had been nervous about changing things, mixing things up a bit, but she had never expected it to turn out like this. She had thought she would have more control, and yet here she was, stuck in the same dilemma that always plagued her when change was involved. Her life spun out of control, and she was left struggling to pick up the pieces.

What had happened to her resolve? What happened to the decision, if somewhat tentative, to take charge and not let the change control her? Why was she once again left feeling torn apart and scared?

Jackie wiped her eyes and took a deep breath. She had a choice. She could mourn the fact that things hadn't turned out as she had intended and continue to live as a passive, timid woman. Or she could say "enough is enough" and do something about it. Why should she let this situation with Paul control her? Just because he was lost and confused didn't mean she had to be. She could still learn from the experience and figure out the best course of action for herself. She could still take charge. And she could still be happy. It wasn't too late. She pushed herself up and went to blow her nose.

A moment later Jackie was at her kitchen table with a notepad. This time it wasn't about what she wanted to change; it was about what she had to change for her sanity. First on the list: find a job. Actually...She scratched out "job" and wrote "career." It wasn't about just paying the bills anymore. She wanted to find something that fulfilled her. While she had enjoyed working in the doctor's office, taking care of the children and organizing the office, she wanted something more. True, it was easy to write it on a notepad. It would be a lot harder to figure out what it was she wanted to do.

Next on the list came volunteering. She wanted to spend time helping others. Perhaps she could help children, be a big sister or some other such thing. She could even just spend time reading to them at the library. Surely there were many possibilities. And then she could feel like she was contributing something, not just existing.

She paused after that, touching the pen to her lower lip. She was hesitant to put the next item on the list. But if the situation with Paul had taught her anything, it was that she wasn't immune to a man's affections. Obviously she knew that. She had had relationships in the past, dates here and there. But nothing serious since she broke up with her college boyfriend. She had spent long enough acting like a spinster. She wanted to feel loved, cherished. She wanted to be in a relationship. And though it was another thing that was easier said than done, she had to put it on the list. Perhaps eventually she could get married, have children. Long ago it had been her intention. Why had she given up on it? Before she lost her nerve, Jackie scribbled her intentions on the notepad. She had to give it a shot.

Three things might not seem like a lot, but seeing the items she had written gave Jackie more than enough to panic about. With a deep breath, she ripped off the sheet of paper and put it to the side. It was time to brainstorm.

Chapter 19

Paul lay in bed, staring at the ceiling. Early morning light filtered through the blinds, and he turned toward it. He was surprised he had slept at all, though it had been very little. The previous day's events weighed heavily on his mind. So much loss in a single day. How would he get past it? But even he had to acknowledge that life was life, and time would make the pain ease if not disappear. He and Pam would get divorced. Uncle Bill's presence would fade. And Jackie would become a woman he had known once, a woman who had changed his life but was part of his past.

He rolled onto his side and gazed at the clock radio on the nightstand. It was still early, only seven in the morning. Normally he would be up by now, getting ready for the day's activities. But he didn't have to go to work until Monday. There was nothing pressing for him to take care of. He would just be killing time, wandering around the house all day aimlessly. Would this be what his life was now? Would he be forever killing time, just waiting for the days to pass?

He lay in a daze for several minutes, wishing he had the motivation to get up and do something, anything. Eventually his stomach rumbled, and he realized he should probably get up and make breakfast. At least it gave him something to do.

Somewhere between the scrambled eggs and the toast his thoughts began to make sense. He was alone now. Unfortunate, yes. Depressing, yes. But that didn't mean his life was over. Hadn't he thought way back before this whole Jackie fiasco that his real problem was the fact that he wasn't comfortable with his own company? Maybe instead of wallowing in this sea of self-pity he should take this time to really figure out what he wanted. And this time, he would make sure he didn't get so distracted. The idea had made him miserable before, but he was already miserable. He might as well be productive while he was being miserable. Who knew? Maybe he would actually get somewhere instead of taking yet another step backward.

Jackie rolled out of bed somewhere after ten and was shocked to see the clock. Then again, she had been up until after midnight. And the emotional roller coaster of the previous day had been exhausting. Still, she had made some progress with her brainstorming the night before, and there was actually a flicker of hope somewhere in her gut. She was tired of being a victim, of struggling with the upheaval that any change brought to her life. It was time to take charge. She would chock up the past month's experiences to a learning opportunity.

Swinging her legs over the side of the bed, Jackie got up and prepared for the day. She had some research to do. The lists of job possibilities and volunteer possibilities that she had compiled needed to be sorted and looked into. Her finances needed to be evaluated. And perhaps, if she was feeling up to it, she would start looking into online dating sites as well, though the thought turned the flicker of hope in her gut to the flapping wings of about a dozen butterflies.

This was good, she thought. She could do this. She was always taking charge of the office at work. Why not take charge of something that really mattered -- her own life? Surely the skills must be transferable.

The newspaper's classifieds weren't too promising, and the online listings weren't much better. But Jackie tried not to get discouraged and decided to update her resume and do general research instead. She had to know not only what her options were, but also what requirements they had, should she decide to go for something new.

Her list of job ideas had included the tried-and-true office work, but she had also racked her brain thinking of other, different, options as well. Her love of children led her to list childcare provider and teacher. She had even gone so far as to list foster parent, though that idea had come a bit later in the evening, as her eyes were drooping. Books led her to librarian and working in a bookstore; cooking led her to working in a restaurant. The unfortunate part was that many of her ideas required additional education. That was where evaluating her finances came into play. Not only did she need to know where she stood -- and how long she could survive if she didn't find a job right away -- but she also needed to know what she could afford, should she decide to go back to school. While she had a college degree, the coursework she had pursued to get a business degree wasn't going to help her much if she decided to become a teacher, librarian or chef. But even if she could afford to go to school, she needed to know what she would go for.

It was a vicious circle, really, and it all came down to what she wanted. She would have to do a lot of soul-searching over the next couple of days to really get a handle on it.

It would be difficult when she went back to work. She didn't know what to expect from her interactions with Paul, and she was afraid of getting sucked back into the drama.

But she had a couple of days until then. Perhaps she could come up with some decisions. Perhaps she could actually move forward instead of barely treading water, afraid she would drown. Perhaps by Monday she would have some answers instead of a growing mountain of questions.

Perhaps by then she would know what it was that she wanted.

Chapter 20

For the first time ever, Paul had counted down the hours until Monday. He arrived at the office well before they opened, grateful to have something to do.

He was reviewing patient files when he heard the front door open. A quick peek down the hall found Jackie entering the waiting room, then turning into the office. He let her hang up her coat in the front closet and put her lunch in the refrigerator in the break room before approaching.

"Good morning, Jackie."

Jackie looked up at him. "Good morning."

"How was your weekend?"

"Fine. How was yours?"

"Fine."

They stared at each other for a moment.

"Well, I guess I'll let you get to work, then."

Paul returned to his office and leaned against the door frame with a sigh of his own. He had lied. His weekend hadn't been fine. It had been a struggle to face himself each morning, and it had been a struggle to fill the waking hours. The days and months ahead suddenly seemed very long, and he didn't know what he was going to do with his time.

Sadly he hadn't gotten very far with getting in touch with himself. The crumpled list that he had written out what seemed like years ago didn't offer much inspiration. He acknowledged that many of the things he had wanted to do were simply rebellion against Pam and her rules. If that wasn't juvenile enough, he found himself feeling like a kindergartener on the first day of school: lost and unsure, without any friends. Any acquaintances he had were back home, an hour away. And even they hadn't been close. Most of the people Paul spent any time with were coworkers or friends of Pam's. It was a sad commentary on what his life had become.

So he had decided to come up with some hobbies. He had gone to a gaming store in a nearby town, thinking that the role-playing games he had enjoyed in high school and college might still be appealing. What he found was a bunch of kids shopping and rolling dice. He felt old. There had to be guys his own age who liked that kind of thing. But how could he find them?

Then he had gone to a bookstore, hoping to pick up some light reading to at least help him pass the time. But it had been so long since he had had free time he didn't even know most of the authors on the bestseller lists. He had picked up a couple that sounded interesting, but he didn't know how far that would get him.

His one success had been at the gym. He joined a local fitness club and decided to sign up with a personal trainer. He could stand to get in shape, and perhaps the exercise would help his mood, as well. Supposedly working out released endorphins, and he could certainly use a few of those these days.

The trainer had been pleasant but strict, and Paul had high hopes that at least a few hours of his week would be spent in an enjoyable activity, being productive at the same time. Maybe he would even meet some people while he was there. Did guys take classes? Or was that a girl thing? He'd have to look into it.

But in the meantime he had a workday to get through. He looked forward to working, to spending the time with his patients. His only concern was interacting with Jackie. He had felt he should break the ice, greet her before the day had really begun. She hadn't seemed happy to see him, not that he could blame her. It would be difficult getting through the next few days or weeks before she left, but he didn't mind. It was better than the alternative, that being her gone. Maybe he could change her mind in the meantime. While he didn't have high hopes of getting her to remain an employee, he still held out hope that he could convince her to be a friend. He could really use one. And, that aside, he truly liked Jackie.

He enjoyed spending time with her, and getting her take on things. He had fond memories of their road trip, and the support she had provided when Uncle Bill had his heart attack. He would have to see what he could do.

But first he had patients to see. It would be a busy day. The office had been closed for a week, and they had understandably gotten a little behind. He was fortunate that another doctor in the area had been able to cover for him and take the sick patients in the meantime. Now he just had to worry about the regular checkups and anything that had come up while he was out. It shouldn't be a bad day at all.

Jackie was having a terrible day. She was grateful to be back at work, since it gave her something other than her life changes to focus on. But it was definitely an adjustment working for Paul. Not that he was a bad boss. It was just awkward going to him. She had thought she could avoid him for the most part, yet she had neglected to remember the hundred times a day she had had to go to Dr. Collins with questions or information regarding patients and the office. Paul was the boss now. He would be the one to talk to. She held off as much as possible, but she couldn't put it off forever, especially when children's health was at stake. She certainly wasn't that selfish. And besides, she had said she could be a professional. She had to at least be true to her word.

He grinned when she entered his office at midday. She was definitely not expecting that. Was she missing something?

"I need you to review these payments and this patient's chart."

"Okay." He held out a hand for the paperwork, then gestured for her to have a seat across from him.

"I'm fine, thanks. You can just leave them on my desk when you're through. I'll be in the break room eating lunch."

"Mind if I join you? I can review these afterward."

Jackie hesitated, then shrugged. It wasn't as if she could refuse him space in his own break room. "Suit yourself."

They entered the room together. Jackie retrieved her lunch from the refrigerator, then sat down and began eating her salad. After popping his frozen entree in the microwave, Paul sat across from her. They sat in awkward silence for a few minutes until the microwave beeped. When Paul got up to get his lunch Jackie released a deep breath. It looked like it was destined to be a long, awkward lunch.

Paul paused with his back facing Jackie. "You know, I knew it would be difficult working together, but I didn't expect you to act so...I don't know...cold."

Jackie looked at him in surprise. Never had she been accused of being cold before. True, she wasn't the most outgoing person, but she certainly wasn't cold. She would like to think she was caring, warm-hearted. "Excuse me?"

He turned to face her. "I guess I just expected you to be more like you were when we first met: shy, quiet." He shrugged. "Now it just seems like you're going out of your way to act indifferent."

Paul brought his lunch over to the table and sat down. Jackie could only gawk.

"That's why I wanted to have lunch together. I hoped we could clear the air."

"I thought we did that the other night."

"We did, I guess." Paul sighed. "I guess it just doesn't feel resolved to me."

"I'm sorry?"

He shrugged again. "Nothing to be sorry about. You said your piece. I guess part of me was still hoping we could be friends after all this. I've come to the realization that I don't have many friends, and while part of what we went through was awkward, I'd like to think that there were a lot of good times, too."

"There were."

"Then what do you say? Any chance we could be friends? I promise I won't make any moves or put you in any awkward positions."

Jackie played with her salad. She wasn't sure how it would make her feel to be friends with him. She had thought a clean break would be best, easiest. And it probably would be. Was he trying to charm her? Was he just lonely? She could certainly understand the latter. She imagined it would be difficult to uproot your life as he had and be left alone. She had her share of lonely moments, and she had friends and acquaintances to socialize with. Paul likely had no one. But did that mean she should put herself in that position?

"Can I think about it?"

Paul nodded enthusiastically. "Of course. I know it's not easy, and that I'm asking a lot. I just...I like you, Jackie." He put up a hand. "As a friend, nothing more. I enjoyed spending time with you, and since you won't be working here anymore, it would be nice to be able to call you once in a while and maybe catch a cup of coffee."

Jackie longed to be on more secure footing. "Have you hired my replacement yet?"

Paul leaned back in his chair. "Not technically. We'll probably hire the woman who was temping, but I had hoped you would be settled before we offered her the job."

"That's very thoughtful of you, but I've evaluated my finances, and I'll be fine. It's not fair to keep her on hold."

"I suppose."

"You should offer her the job. At the very least you need to know if she wants it. If not, you'll have to start advertising. And if she does want it, we'll need to get her trained."

"Okay. I know you're right. I guess it just seemed so final."

"It is final, Paul."

"I know." He sighed. "Okay. I'll call her this afternoon."

"Great."

"How long do you think it will take to train her?"

"Probably not long. She did work here for a couple of weeks. She knows how the office runs."

"True."

They ate in silence for a few moments. Jackie was grateful. She just wanted to get back to work and move past this awkward lunch.

"So have you decided what you're going to do yet?"

Jackie sighed. "I've got some ideas. I'm just weighing my options to determine the best course of action."

Paul grinned. "You're gonna cook, huh?"

Jackie shrugged. "It's one of the things I've thought about -- working in a restaurant, that is. But I would need training and education, and I don't know if that's the best option right now. But I'm considering it."

"I think you should go for it."

Jackie looked up and met Paul's gaze. "Not all of us are comfortable uprooting our lives, Paul. I tend to be a little more cautious."

"Trust me, this was unusual for me, too. I tend to be a little more cautious, too. But some things you don't have a choice over. And sometimes you just need to take a chance."

"We'll see."

"Of course you could always stay here and work for me. It could be fun. And you could make your decisions later."

"You know that's not happening."

"But it could. We'd –"

"Enough, Paul!" Jackie stood up abruptly. "I have enough to worry about without you sending me on a guilt trip. You are a grown man. Start acting like it."

Paul's head reared back as though he had been slapped, then he watched her as she packed up her lunch and left the break room.

Jackie returned to her desk and tossed her lunch bag in a drawer. She had intended to review her lists from the weekend over lunch, but they hadn't left her purse. And why? Because Paul had dominated her thoughts. Again. Perhaps she would have a few spare moments in the afternoon to look them over.

Jackie took a deep breath and, after a moment, calmed down. She couldn't blame Paul entirely. She was on edge these days, unsure of herself. She really had to start making some decisions. She had never been one to procrastinate, and yet here she was focusing more on making lists and coming up with ideas than actually coming up with solutions. Apparently when it came to big life decisions she was a bit less efficient. And she didn't like it one bit.

It took Paul a moment to absorb what Jackie had said, and when he did, he wasn't happy. She was right. What had he become? He was practically begging her to be his friend, asking her to stay here, pestering her about her life changes. Not only was that not fair to her, but where was his pride? He was acting like a whiny brat, and that wasn't who he wanted to be.

After about ten minutes of moping Paul sat up straight in his chair. What was wrong with him? Was he so desperate that he had to practically beg Jackie to be in his life? He used to be a confident, honorable man. And even if most of their friends had been Pam's, he had been able to hold his own in conversations. He had plenty to offer. Why was he acting like he didn't? Sure, it was harder to make friends at this stage in the game. But he figured the same rule probably applied for friends as it did for relationships: you had to love yourself before someone else could love you. In all honesty, what did he actually have to offer Jackie? He was a broken, disheartened man who was desperate for human contact -- and acted like it. Maybe it was time he learned to stand on his own two feet again. And this time he wouldn't put forth some two-bit effort; he would be his own person and discover who he was and what he wanted.

After a moment with his new resolution, Paul emerged from the break room and made his way to Jackie's desk. She looked up warily.

"Can I help you?"

"I'm sorry, Jackie."

"There's nothing to be sorry about."

"Yes, there is. I've been a selfish, needy jerk, and I put you on the spot unnecessarily. Thank you for having the courage to put me in my place. I really needed that."

Jackie blushed. "I don't know if I really 'put you in your place,' as you put it."

"Of course you did. As you should have. It's been a rough couple of months, and I'm still working on getting my footing. But I was wrong to rely so heavily on you. I'm going to take this opportunity to discover who I am."

"Isn't that what the road trip was supposed to do?"

"Yeah," he admitted bashfully. "But I don't think I was really ready for it. Otherwise I don't think I would have gotten so easily sidetracked."

"Well, then, I hope it works this time."

"Me, too. I'm sick and tired of being a miserable mess."

"Good luck."

"Thanks." He flashed her a grin, then returned to his office to review his next patient's file.

The file didn't take long to review, and as he perused the file, he thought about how pleased he was with his decision to take over the practice. Even before Uncle Bill had passed away, he had enjoyed working with the kids. They were so different from adults, and most of them were a joy to work with. At least it was one positive change he had made.

Working with children made him regret, however, the decision he and Pam had made to not start a family. Maybe if he ever remarried he should look for someone who wanted to have kids. It was something to think about, anyway. What would it feel like to have a tiny life in your hands? To watch that life grow and develop over time, to mold that little life and discover the person who existed within? It must be an awesome feeling, Paul mused. And it was a feeling he decided he wanted to experience.

But before he could mold and shape a child's life, he really needed to take the time to mold and shape his own. As it stood it was a mess. He was in no condition to be a role model for an impressionable little boy or girl, and if he needed to use that image as motivation, then that's what he would do.

Paul went home that night and sat in his living room, staring at a dark TV screen. It didn't matter if anything was on; he wouldn't be paying attention to it anyway. His mind had been running a mile a minute since his encounter with Jackie earlier that day. He had to learn to be comfortable with himself. So here he was, sitting by himself, in a quiet room. It didn't take long to get bored. But the sad part was: he didn't even know what he wanted to do. He could turn on the TV, but that wouldn't ease the boredom. It was just something to do to pass the time.

He felt lost, confused. There wasn't anything fulfilling he could think of to do. Anything he thought of was just as bad as watching TV.

Maybe he should make another list, he mused. Perhaps he could determine what he wanted to do. Maybe he could even determine where he wanted to go from here.

With some effort Paul pushed himself off the couch and went in search of paper and a pencil. A minute later he sank back onto the sofa and placed the pad of paper on his lap.

He intended to make a list; he really did. But before he even processed what he was doing, his words turned into a journal entry instead. He found himself pouring out his thoughts and feelings. When he realized what he was doing he was almost ripped the paper up in disgust. It was so...girlie. The only thing that stopped him was the realization that he felt better. It was a relief to get his thoughts on paper. He didn't have to constantly go over them in his head; he had them right in front of him.

In simple black and white he had poured out his feelings about Pam divorcing him, Uncle Bill dying, feeling alone and lost and confused. About taking over the practice he was grateful. About Jackie he was a bit conflicted. Nothing was resolved, but by getting it all down on paper he felt as if a weight had been lifted. It had been a strange, unfortunate set of circumstances. It would take him a while to truly get over them. But perhaps now that he had really acknowledged them he could move past them. He could stand on his own two feet.

And he was starting by figuring out who he wanted to be.

Paul tore off the pages he had scribbled his journal entry on. He wasn't sure if he should keep them or not, but for now he would put them aside. As he sat staring at a blank sheet of paper he thought about the man he wanted to be. What did his future hold? What did he want it to hold?

He found himself thinking about Uncle Bill. They were a lot alike, especially now that Paul was alone. Uncle Bill had never remarried after Aunt Sarah had passed away. Perhaps he had never had a desire to. Or perhaps he just felt guilty. Who knew? All Paul knew was that as it stood he would likely end up just like his uncle: happy at work but a little lost and lonely when it came to his personal life. Paul couldn't imagine spending the rest of his life alone in this big, empty house. Even if he learned to be comfortable with his own company, he knew there had to be more worthwhile ways to spend his days.

So who did he want to be?

The doctor part was a given. He loved his job, and he enjoyed working with his patients. He knew he needed friends, but he also knew he couldn't force it like he had tried to do with Jackie. That method obviously didn't work. And he didn't want people to feel obligated to be his friend. He was a worthwhile human being, and he deserved friends who actually wanted to spend time with him. Perhaps in time he would be ready to be in another relationship. He didn't want to be alone forever, and as great as friends were, he would definitely love someone to share life's little moments with. Thinking about friends and relationships, though, brought him back to square one: where was he going to meet these people?

He needed hobbies. He had already determined that. The gym held potential, as he needed to get in shape and had enjoyed going. He really should start going more often. But beyond that, he wasn't sure what held appeal.

The more he thought about it, the more the idea of getting active in the community came up. Maybe if he volunteered somewhere or joined a committee in local government he could be productive while meeting new people. That idea had merit. Now he just had to figure out what he wanted to participate in. Clubs? Soup kitchens? Politics?

Paul didn't care much for politics overall, but local government wasn't bad. He could see himself on a committee to beautify the town center or some other such thing. Perhaps economic development. That sounded good, actually. And as a new business owner in town, he should probably join the chamber of commerce as well. He scribbled the ideas on his notepad.

The idea of giving back held appeal, too. Maybe while he was over at town hall looking into joining the economic development committee he could inquire about local organizations that could use help. He wrote that down.

Paul grinned. He was feeling really good about this. At least he felt like he was making some progress, instead of being stuck at home bemoaning his fate. He could see himself now: a distinguished older gentleman, loving wife at his side, receiving some award or other for his involvement in the community. Wouldn't that be nice? And maybe it wasn't too late to have a couple of kids who would sit in the audience and look up proudly at their old man. What would that feel like? His heart clenched at the thought. After so many years of assuming he would never be a father, he was astonished to find how much he really wanted to be. Now he just had to find someone to start that family with.

Jackie had gone over the incident with Paul a million times. What had possessed her to act like that? She really should apologize. While she knew it needed to be said, she should have found a more delicate way of approaching the subject. She would discuss it with Paul tomorrow.

Until then, however, she would feel bad.

What was with her lately? She was feeling uncharacteristically feisty. She was usually subdued, gentle. Now she was tempted to destroy her front closet, yell at Paul, and say "to hell with it" about aspects of her life she had until now held dear. She wanted to throw caution to the wind and try something new. She wanted to change everything about everything.

But there was still that darn fear that was holding her back. And she didn't know if she should let the fear remind her of who she was or try to push it back and become a new person.

Was it really necessary to change everything? Perhaps just a small change or two would be enough to satisfy her without making her feel as if she had completely surrendered her old self.

What a mess. Jackie didn't know what to think or feel anymore. If she was truly honest with herself, she had to admit that her life before had been boring. She had liked her job, but had it really fulfilled her? She was good at it. She was efficient, responsible, friendly. But it didn't challenge her. She knew what she was doing, and she did it. Perhaps that was why she was so afraid of change: because she didn't know what she was doing. But she had to admit there was a little thrill in it, too. Who knew what the future held? She could be anything, do anything.

Then again, having too many options was a problem in and of itself. She didn't know where to begin. The list she had made was a start, yes, but she was still as lost as ever.

Maybe she had been too hasty with Paul. She could really use someone to talk about this with. She thought about turning to Mary, but Mary had enough on her plate, with being pregnant and everything. Mary didn't need to hear about her mid-life crisis, or whatever this was. But Paul...he was going through the same thing. And he had seen parts of her on their road trip that she hadn't shown anyone. He knew about her interest in food and cooking. She had moved past some of her fears for that trip.

The next morning Jackie walked into the office, put away her purse, coat and lunch, then went in search of Paul. She found him already in his office, reviewing files.

He looked up when she knocked on the door. "Hey," he greeted her with a grin.

"Hi."

"How are you this morning?"

"I'm fine." Jackie paused for a moment. "Look, Paul, I'm sorry for yesterday. I was abrupt and rude, and there was no reason for that."

Paul waved her away. "Don't worry about it. You actually did me a favor. It's about time I acknowledged how much of a whiny pain in the ass I've been." He grinned again.

Jackie blushed. "It's not that. I just –. I don't know what. But I feel badly about how I approached the subject, and to make matters worse, I think I may have been too hasty. Things might be a little awkward, but I think we could help each other. Being friends wouldn't be so bad."

Paul shook his head. "Nope. You were right. I need to be able to stand on my own two feet. I need to figure out who I am, without you or Uncle Bill or Pam to be a crutch. I've got some plans in the works, and I'm really looking forward to it."

"Oh." Jackie didn't know what to think. Now that she wanted to be Paul's friend, he wanted nothing to do with her. Now what?

"I think it'll be good for you, too. You can figure out all those decisions you had to make without me screwing things up."

Maybe that's what she was afraid of. If Paul stood on his own two feet, she'd have to, too. But since when did she back away from a challenge? Taking a deep breath, Jackie straightened her back. "You're right. I was right. I'm sorry. My brain is just a bit of a jumbled mess right now. I had thought it would help to talk to someone about it."

Paul gestured toward the chair across from his desk. "You can still talk to me. We agreed to be a support group, remember? How about as long as you still work for me, you can talk to me about this stuff? After that, we'll just go our separate ways."

Jackie swallowed. That was when things would get the most difficult, but she would take what she could get. "Okay."

Paul grinned again. "Great. Have a seat."

Even as she spoke, Jackie was propping herself on the edge of the chair. "Don't we have to get to work?"

"First appointment's not until 10. I'm afraid I've lost a few patients. But it'll be fine. So what did you want to talk about?"

Jackie didn't know how much to say. How did she put into words what she was feeling? And how much should she really share with him? "Well, I probably shouldn't admit this, but I still don't know what I'm going to do for a job."

"You've still got a couple of weeks. You'll come up with something. Have you looked into the cooking thing?"

Jackie couldn't answer the question; she had locked in on the first part of what he said. "A couple of weeks? We have a date?"

"Oh, yes, sorry. I actually just found out this morning. Monica has taken the position." Monica was the woman who had filled in for her. "I figured she'd start on Monday, and you could spend a couple of weeks training her. If you need more time, though, I'm sure we could accommodate. I've talked to the other women in the office. I didn't realize quite how much you do around here. I'm sure it'll take a while to train."

Jackie found herself blushing. "Yes, well. Things happen." After a moment she swallowed hard. Things really were happening. Her replacement had been hired. A couple of weeks, and she was out on the street.

Paul seemed to notice her panicked emotions. "There's no rush, Jackie. You can take as long as you need. You know I like having you around."

Jackie could only manage a nod. She closed her eyes, took a deep breath and forced herself to smile. "It's okay. Two weeks should be fine."

"Are you sure?"

"Of course." She forced another smile. "It's not fair to make you pay for two people to do the work of one."

"I'm not worried about that."

"It's okay. Really." She would make it be okay. What choice did she have? She had made her bed. Now she had to lie in it.

"Okay. So, anyway, what ideas have you had for a job?"

"Nothing that's stuck so far. I guess part of the problem is that I don't know where to start. Regardless of what kind of job I choose to go with, I'll be starting from scratch. And I don't know how to begin. It's been a while since I took on something new."

"I would imagine." He shot her a grin.

"I might actually take some time to figure things out. I have some money saved up, and I would love to take some continuing education classes. Maybe something will appeal to me." She had had the thought before, but now that she said it aloud, she realized how appealing it sounded. She had evaluated her finances; she had enough saved without tapping her retirement fund to get her by for seven months, as long as she didn't overdo it. Even if she took a month or two to figure things out, that should give her plenty of time to find a job. She hoped. Winter classes would be starting soon. Not working would give her plenty of time to take as many as she wanted. She could use her last couple of paychecks to pay for the courses. Would it work? She had no way of knowing. But a little spark was coming to life low in her belly that was beginning to feel suspiciously like excitement. When was the last time she was really excited about anything? Of course there had been the road trip...but she wasn't letting herself think about that. This plan was right. She could feel it.

"That sounds great. I hope you find something you can be passionate about, even if it's not cooking."

"At this point I don't know what to expect, but I always have this kind of work to fall back on, so if nothing pans out, I won't be completely without options." And at least in the meantime she would enjoy herself, do what she actually wanted to do, and maybe learn something in the process.

"I'm sure you'll be successful. And I'm glad to hear you have a game plan."

"Yes, well, it's a bit rough around the edges right now, but hopefully it'll work out. I'm kind of flying by the seat of my pants right now, and I'm not used to it."

"At least the road trip prepared you a little bit for that."

Jackie gave Paul a small smile. "Yes, I suppose it did." After a moment Jackie stood up. "Well, I guess I should get to work. Don't want my boss to yell at me." She smiled again.

"Yeah, I hear he's a real slave driver." Paul returned the smile, and Jackie left the office.

It had been nice to talk to Paul, but she had a feeling this would be the last time they would really talk like this. Their relationship was bound to taper off as they went their separate ways, and with no real friendship to tie them together, conversation would likely consist of banalities until Jackie left the office. It was sad, but just the way life was, she supposed. At least she still had Mary and her other book club friends. And there was always the opportunity to make more, especially once she started taking classes. When one door closes, another door opens, right? Perhaps this was just the door closing on this chapter of her life. Who knew what the next chapter would bring?

Chapter 21

DECEMBER

Jackie brushed a strand of hair from her eyes and stirred the contents of the pot in front of her. The soup kitchen was bustling today, but that wasn't a surprise. While it had always been a popular choice for the local homeless, she was under the impression that things had really picked up since she had taken over the kitchen. Apparently she had a knack for cooking decent food in bulk. Who knew?

"Hey, Jackie, is that stew about done? The natives are getting restless."

Jackie looked up to find the kitchen's manager, Susan, peering into the kitchen through the window looking over the dining room. "Yeah, it's good to go."

"Great." Susan disappeared for a moment, then reappeared at the kitchen door. Grabbing a couple of pot holders, she lifted the pot from the stove and returned to the dining room.

Jackie wiped her brow. It had been three weeks since she started volunteering at the soup kitchen, and so far she was enjoying it. She had found her days were empty, since most of the continuing education classes took place at night or on the weekends to accommodate working folk. So she had decided to take the opportunity to volunteer. She figured cooking at a soup kitchen would serve a dual purpose: help her community and give her a taste of what being a chef was all about.

The menu was simple, though she had dressed it up a bit in the short time she had been there. There were few fancy ingredients; most of what they used was donated. But she enjoyed it. The people were nice, hard-working men and women who really cared about the people they served. And in the short time she had worked there, the others had pretty much turned over the kitchen to her. Since she had a genuine interest in cooking – and ideas on not only what to serve but how to prepare it – they determined she was the best choice for head chef. She had to admit it gave her a little bubble of satisfaction to be looked up to by her peers.

It had been a month since she had left the doctor's office, but she hadn't let herself dawdle. In addition to a few classes and volunteering at the soup kitchen, she had been helping at the local social services department preparing meal baskets and gifts for needy residents in the area. Thanksgiving had kept her hopping, and Christmas was right around the corner. She expected to be busy right up to the time she left to see her parents on Christmas Eve. She certainly wasn't complaining, though. She had never felt so alive, so fulfilled. Not only was she good at what she was doing; she was also helping others and really making a difference in her community. And she enjoyed it. Overall, it was a wonderful situation. The only problem was: she wasn't getting paid. Ah, if only she could fall in love with a rich man so she could devote her life to helping others. Jackie chuckled to herself and dug out another pot to get more stew going. They would need some for the dinner crowd.

Around four o'clock she turned over her apron to the dinner chef. She had a class to get to. Tonight was her journaling class, and she was looking forward to it. Though it was only the third class, she had already found that she enjoyed putting pen to paper. It had been liberating to get her thoughts down, and she was learning much about herself in the process. She hoped that through her journaling she would be able to make connections in her mind that would lead her to her life's work. It was worth a shot anyway. What did she have to lose?

The holiday fair was coming together nicely, if Paul did say so himself. He had opted to join the Economic Development Commission, and his first project was to organize a holiday crafts and gifts fair for local businesses to promote their wares. They were taking over the parks and recreation department's gymnasium, and he and his crew had spent the past three hours disguising the basketball hoops and bleachers to create a holiday bazaar. There would be a guy dressed up as Santa handing out candy canes, and a raffle when shoppers first walked in. The local women's club had organized a bake sale, and the Kiwanis club was setting up craft stations for the kids. If it was half as successful as Paul anticipated, the fair would be an asset to the town. It was drawing visitors to the town center and showcasing many businesses in the area. All in all it should be a great time, and he was proud of his involvement.

On a personal note, organizing the fair had given him the opportunity to connect with several local residents and possibly begin a few friendships. He had already gotten a couple of new patients from the deal. And he had had a lot of fun.

Paul had never been one to shy away from hard work, but he had never taken on a project quite like this one. He found he enjoyed it. He enjoyed organizing and planning. When he and Pam were together, Pam had done all the party planning, shopping, organizing. Any ideas he had were brushed aside in favor of Pam's game plan already in the works. For once he had gotten to see his ideas come to fruition. It was a nice feeling, and he found it very fulfilling.

Not to mention it filled his evenings.

Nights and weekends were the hardest. He found himself wandering around the house aimlessly, bored and listless. Having committee meetings to attend, fair supplies to buy, and decorations to make, had helped fill those vast hours. It got his brain working and gave him the opportunity to be creative. He loved it.

And he had to admit that seeing it all come together was amazing. The gymnasium was transformed. It was like a winter wonderland. He had toyed with the idea of having the volunteers dress up as elves, but that would mean he would have to, too. And there was only so far his holiday spirit would extend. Especially this year.

It would be different, that's for sure. The actual day he would likely be heading to his parents' house. But all the time leading up to it? He had no idea. The fair had taken up a lot of his time and attention, but it would be over this weekend, and he still had two more weeks to get through. No new projects were being started, and he had no idea how he would fill up his time. He didn't want to think about Pam and Uncle Bill, and he was afraid that's what would happen. He hadn't gotten very far in his quest for hobbies. He would probably have to start looking for something before he went crazy. This time of year it shouldn't be hard to find something to do. Perhaps he could volunteer somewhere. He could deliver gift baskets or something. He would have to look into it once the fair was over. Until then, he had his hands full.

"Great job, guys. The place looks awesome." He patted the back of his second-in-command Joan. "I'd say we're all ready for the fair tomorrow."

"I agree," Joan said with a nod. "You did a great job, Paul."

"*We* did a great job," he countered. "The first annual Munsen Holiday Fair is destined to be a success."

The committee broke up and headed for the door, but Paul lingered. He didn't really have anywhere to go at the moment, and it made him proud to see what the group had accomplished. His thoughts were already moving to next year, to ideas he had for the fair's second event. Yes, he knew he was getting ahead of himself, but it was better than the alternative. The more he could keep his mind off the trials of the season, the better. Once the new year got started, then he could focus on new projects, such as the farmer's market the commission was talking about putting on. He could definitely get behind that. But until then...well, he had to keep himself busy. He already knew that.

Maybe Monday on his lunch break he would swing by the town hall and touch base with the social services department. Maybe they would need help with food or gift deliveries. He had the time. Might as well use it to do some good.

Chapter 22

Mondays were holiday gift days. People shopping over the weekend tended to flood the department with gifts on Monday mornings, and Jackie was on hand to take donations with open arms.

The generosity of others never ceased to amaze her, especially at this time of year, when so many had such high expenses. It was nice that people who had plenty of excuses could still scrape up a few dollars – or much more – to help their fellow man.

That Monday morning was no exception. The drop box outside the department was filled, and shortly after the doors opened, additional bags and boxes started arriving. Toys, clothes, food – Jackie spent the next couple of hours sorting the goodies and prepping them for the next step. It was exhausting work, and by the time twelve o'clock rolled around, Jackie was ready for lunch. She was just about to step out when a bell chimed indicating someone had entered the front office lobby.

Expecting someone else bringing in gifts, Jackie plastered a smile on her face and left the back room. To her surprise she found Paul standing in the waiting area.

"Paul?"

He looked up to meet her gaze. "Jackie?"

"What are you doing here?"

"I could say the same about you! I stopped by to look into volunteer opportunities."

"Not a great time, unfortunately. Just about everybody has gone out to lunch. I was about to leave myself."

"Oh." His face fell.

"What were you looking to do?"

"Well, I figured with the holidays that maybe there were gift baskets I could deliver or something."

"There have been a ton of donations. I'm sure they could use the help. Do you want me to have someone give you a call?"

"That would be great."

"Okay."

They stood in awkward silence for a few moments before Jackie gestured toward the back room. "I was just about to grab my purse and go out for lunch. Would you like to join me?"

Paul's face lit up. "I would love that."

They walked to the front door of the town hall in silence. There was a deli down the street that Jackie sometimes went to, and she steered them in that direction. After a couple of minutes had passed, she turned to look at Paul. "So how have you been?"

"I've been great. Keeping busy. How about you?"

"I'm doing very well. I'm taking some classes and doing some volunteer work. I'm enjoying it so far."

"You seem very...relaxed."

Jackie smiled. "I am, surprisingly. I thought I would be stressing about money and about my job decision, but I'm doing pretty well."

"Any luck with the job hunt?"

"I've had some ideas, but they would all require schooling, so I may need to find something temporary."

"Going to cooking school?"

Jackie shook her head. "No, I don't think so."

Paul raised his eyebrows. "No?"

"Nah. I'm taking a cooking class now, and while I enjoy it, I think the structure and hoity-toityness of it would kill the joy for me."

Paul laughed. "Hoity-toityness?"

Jackie grinned. "Yeah. You know. You go to a fancy restaurant, and the portion is the size of a quarter, but the presentation is all elaborate. I'd rather just make good food that people enjoy."

"You wouldn't have to be all fancy."

She shrugged. "I guess not, but the school would probably train that way."

"I suppose."

"Besides, what I'm doing now suits me better."

"What are you doing now?"

"Cooking in a soup kitchen."

"Really? I'm impressed."

"I don't know how impressive it is, but I enjoy it. The staff is great, and the clientele really seems to enjoy what I make."

"They can't really afford to be picky."

"True. But attendance has gone up since I've taken over the kitchen. I'm taking that as a good sign."

"As you should." They arrived at the deli then, and Paul held the door open for her. Conversation lulled as they ordered and found a seat. As Paul unwrapped his sandwich, he began again. "I'm glad to hear you're happy. It's a shame volunteer work doesn't pay, huh?"

Jackie sighed. "If only. Though one of the things I'm considering would still be helping others."

"Oh yeah? What's that?"

"I'm thinking of going into social work. I'd like to try for DCF kind of stuff, working with kids."

"Commendable. It can be very trying, though."

"I know. That's the only thing holding me back. I don't know how I would handle some of the situations these kids have to deal with. Abusive parents and all that."

"I'm sure you would learn how to deal with that. It wouldn't be easy, but, sadly, you get used to it. And think of all the good you could do."

"I know." She sighed. "It's something to think about anyway." Jackie picked up her fork and poked at her salad. "But enough about me. How have you been?"

"Good. Business is good. I've gotten a few new patients to replace those that left."

"That's good. I started getting worried for a bit there. It seemed like you were losing quite a few."

He shrugged. "It wasn't as many as it seemed. But we're almost up to the same number now."

"Great."

"Yeah."

"What else have you been up to?"

"Well, I've started participating in local government."

"Really? Wow."

"Yeah. I joined the Economic Development Commission, and I've worked on some projects with them. I led the committee for the gift fair this past weekend."

"I heard about that. I wanted to stop by, but I had a prior commitment. How did it go?"

"Really well. We're hoping to make it an annual event. But the work for this year is done. That's why I'm looking to do some volunteering. Everything is winding down for the holidays."

"Everything except gift drives!" Jackie grinned again. "We've been hopping. The past couple of weeks I've been so busy, it's a good thing I didn't have a job."

"I'm sure they appreciate the help."

Jackie nodded. "They definitely do. And I'm happy to do it. Especially these days, it's nice to know there are still people who want to help others."

Silence fell again, but it was companionable. They each made progress on their sandwiches and looked around the bustling deli.

It felt strange to sit with him like this, Jackie thought. Their time together seemed forever ago, and yet here they were, less than a month later. It was amazing how much had changed in that month. She felt like a different person. She had thought she would flounder without the structure of an office job, and yet here she was, enjoying the ride. Her classes challenged her; her volunteer work fulfilled her. It was a shame she couldn't go on like this forever. But what she had told Paul was true: she had had some insight into her potential career, and the thought that she could help people for a living really appealed to her. Yes, it would be difficult seeing some of the things these kids went through, but it went on whether she saw it or not. At least being involved she could do something about it. With that resolved, she decided to start looking into social work degrees. Jackie smiled.

"What's the smile for?"

"Huh?" Jackie turned to look at Paul.

"You smiled. Any particular reason?"

"Not really. It's just sitting here with you is so surreal, and yet talking to you has helped solidify things in my mind. I think I'm going to look into social work programs."

"Good for you. I think it'll be a good fit."

"I hope so. Now I just have to figure out what I'm going to do until I graduate. I can't pay all my bills and a college education with no income."

"Something will come up. And even if you have to take something that's not ideal, at least you know it'll just be temporary."

"True." Jackie balled up the wrapper from her sandwich and tucked it into her salad container. "I think I'm going to head back to the office. Did you want to come back and talk to Janet? She's the coordinator of the holiday program."

"That would be great." Paul stuffed the last bit of sandwich in his mouth and balled up his wrapper as well. A moment later they were on their way.

Jackie got back to work when they returned to the office, while Paul discussed volunteering with Janet. Jackie was just finishing up when Paul popped his head into the sorting room.

"I'm gonna get going, Jackie. It was great seeing you."

Jackie looked up. "You, too. Did Janet have anything for you?"

He nodded. "Yup. I'm helping deliver food baskets and gifts next week."

"I'm glad. I wish I could see the faces of people when they get all this stuff."

"You're welcome to tag along if you want."

Jackie paused. It was tempting, but did she want to start getting involved with Paul again? "I probably won't have the time. But thanks."

Paul seemed to notice her reluctance. "No pressure, Jackie. It was great catching up with you, and I'd love it if we could be friendly, but if you're not comfortable with that, it's okay."

Jackie took a deep breath. "I know. I just…" She looked down at the board games she had just sorted. "I guess I just kind of associate you with confusion and complications. I'm heading in the right direction now, and I don't know how you would factor in."

"Wow. That was blunt."

Jackie blushed. "I'm sorry."

He waved her away. "No, don't be. I understand. It's nice to know you're on more secure footing now."

"I'm getting there, anyway."

"I'm glad."

Paul spent a few moments looking around the room at the gifts stacked on tables and in boxes. "Well, I guess I'd better get going."

"It was good seeing you, Paul."

"Yeah, you, too." He gave her a somewhat sad smile. "Maybe I'll see you around."

With that he was gone, and Jackie released a breath. After taking a minute to compose herself, she gathered up her purse and coat and left the room. She was just closing the door when Mary wandered down the hallway carrying two large bags full of toys.

"Don't tell me I'm too late!"

Jackie pushed the door back open. "This must be my day for visitors."

Mary ducked into the room, and Jackie turned the light back on. "Oh yeah? Who else stopped by?"

"Paul."

"Paul?" It took a moment for Mary to place the name. "Oh yeah, the guy you went on the road trip with."

"That's the one."

"He came to see you? That was sweet."

"He came to volunteer, actually. Seeing me was just a bonus."

"What's he gonna do?"

"Deliver gifts."

"You should tag along."

Jackie sighed. "You think so? He asked me to, but I thought it would be...weird."

Mary shrugged. "It's your call. I've just gotten the feeling that there's something unresolved there. Maybe I'm just reading into things. I've never even met the man."

Jackie sighed again. "No, you're right. Things were awkward when I left, and they're awkward now. We did catch up a bit, though, which was nice. If only we could move past certain things, I think we could be friends. Maybe."

"Then give it a shot. What's the worst that happens? I doubt he's gonna jump your bones while you're out delivering gifts."

"I know. I just...I don't know."

"You know when it's time to do something?"

"When's that?"

"When you've run out of excuses not to."

Chapter 23

Jackie thought about Paul all during the drive home, and while she prepared dinner. Thoroughly fed up with yet another decision to be made concerning Paul, she decided to instead start researching social work programs.

Two hours later she had learned about Bachelor of Social Work programs and found some local colleges that offered them. She could get her Masters degree in one year instead of two if she went with a BSW, and while she didn't know if she wanted to be in school that long, she had to acknowledge that it might be a necessity. Might as well save herself some time and money and do it all in one shot. Now she just had to decide if she really wanted to go for it.

Needing a break, Jackie started casually browsing the internet. She checked her e-mail, browsed recipes, clicked on a few ads for shopping specials. It didn't take long to encounter an ad for an online dating site, and while she would usually ignore it, she found herself floating her cursor above the link. What would it hurt? She had talked about seeking male companionship, but she hadn't done anything about it. Maybe it was time she started looking.

Her heart pounding, butterflies in her stomach, she clicked the ad.

She could browse member profiles without signing up, so she spent some time perusing the offerings, so to speak. It was a strange way to meet people, she decided, but she could see why it was so popular. You could learn about someone without wasting much time. While it might take away from first-date conversation, it could be a useful tool for those not into the whole dating scene –

like herself. Maybe she could find someone with similar interests without having to worry about putting herself out there. She wouldn't have to go to bars and clubs or work up the nerve to introduce herself to someone in a class or group she participated in.

The "join now" button was displayed prominently on each page, but Jackie hesitated before clicking. She had gotten a lot braver since she decided to change her life, but there was something scary about taking this particular leap. It was easy to be brave when you were doing something temporary, like a class or volunteering. If you didn't like it, you could stop. But when it came to a life change such as finding the person you were meant to spend the rest of your life with, it got a little trickier. She had always pictured herself married with children, but how she would meet that man in her life had always remained hazy. It was one of those "always been that way" dreams, without having to think about the awkward dating phase, getting-to-know-you steps, and "will he call again?" insecurities. Was building an online dating profile the first step on this new journey? Or would it just lead to heartache? Well, she hadn't come all this way just to balk at a little online questionnaire. Taking a deep breath, Jackie began to fill in the little boxes.

Paul scolded himself all during the ride home and throughout the evening. Why had he put Jackie on the spot like that? Hadn't he learned his lesson by now? They were leaving that part of their lives behind. Heck, it had been his decision, ultimately. Why was he trying to go back on it now? He had all but forgotten her in the progress his life had made.

Okay, that was a lie. Parts of her had stayed with him, and truth be told, he was glad he had run into her, glad they had had lunch, glad he had invited her along to deliver gifts. He liked her, dammit. But it was obvious that ship had sailed.

After popping a frozen dinner in the microwave, Paul grabbed the newspaper off the kitchen counter and sat at the dining table. He needed a distraction, and while death and destruction weren't exactly uplifting topics, they did take his mind off Jackie's smile.

Once dinner had been consumed, Paul cleaned up, then collapsed in the dining chair again. Distraction aside, he had some decisions to make. Delivering holiday gifts would fill a couple of days, but he really had to decide what he was going to do the rest of the time. If he didn't keep himself busy, he was bound to go crazy. He hoped to get involved in more committee events in the spring, but that left a couple of months with not much on the agenda.

Truth be told, he wasn't looking forward to the holidays. If he could, he would bypass them altogether and skip right to spring. But that was out of his hands, so he had to try and make the best of it. Maybe he would look for other volunteer opportunities. He could ring a bell for the Salvation Army or something.

Once the holidays were over, though, then what? January was notorious for being the most depressing month of the year. This year, especially, with the weight of his grief and the emptiness of this house enveloping him, he didn't know how he would survive.

Paul thought back to Jackie, and how her life had changed. She seemed happy now. Then he thought about how he had to stop thinking about Jackie. Maybe the best way to do that was to meet new people. He could get over Pam and move past Jackie in one fell swoop. It was a thought anyway.

That decided, Paul moved into the room that used to be his uncle's office. The décor hadn't changed much, but Paul had added his computer to the large desk that sat by the window. He sat at that desk now and turned on the laptop. Where should he go? Personal ads? Online dating sites? Chat rooms? He knew there were crazy people out there, but they were probably in all of the above.

He hit up the chat rooms first. He found a couple of forums geared toward professionals in the medical field, and a half hour later decided he had found his new addiction. He was comfortable dealing with medicine, but this gave him the opportunity to meet people, too, even if it was just in cyberspace. At least he didn't feel quite so lonely.

Paul ended up spending two hours chatting with strangers on the net. By the end of the evening, they didn't feel like strangers anymore. They were nice people, and he loved that they could talk about their lives but bring in medical references nonchalantly. They were equals with similar interests. He could get honest input about having his own practice and how it played a part in having – or not having

– a personal life, as opposed to working in a larger office. He could get opinions on dealing with employees, relating to patients, or getting more clients. At the same time he could talk about the hottest restaurants, newest movies, and current sports scores.

By the time Paul went to bed, he was feeling better about things. Talking with others online helped him feel connected. When he was feeling like everyone had abandoned him, that was a difficult feeling to grasp. It was nice to know he now had a place to turn. He even had plans to connect with a couple of the doctors in the forum the following evening. He had to find out how Matt had broken that difficult news to his patient and how Cathy had fared at her malpractice hearing. As his eyes drifted shut, Paul couldn't help but smile. Maybe he would make it through the holidays after all.

Jackie woke up the next morning with butterflies in her stomach. The day ahead of her was nothing out of the ordinary for her, yet she felt nervous and excited at the same time. Had anyone responded to her online profile?

It was still early, she knew. By the time the questionnaire had met her approval and she had found a decent picture to upload, it had been nearly midnight. It was only eight now. But given that others kept different hours than she, perhaps there was a chance someone would have found her among the masses.

Before she checked, though, Jackie forced herself to make a cup of tea and have a couple of pieces of toast. The longer she waited, the greater the chance she wouldn't be disappointed. But she found herself rushing through breakfast anyway.

It wasn't even eight thirty when she booted up her desktop computer. She found herself tapping her fingers on the desk, waiting impatiently for the computer to start up.

The only message waiting for her looked a bit shady, so she deleted it without responding. She had no interest in dating a South African prince.

Discouraged, Jackie decided to take some time to browse the available men instead. She doubted she would contact any of them, but it was nice to get a feel for what was out there. She found many decent-sounding guys, and she had to admit she was tempted to send a message to one or two. But while she had changed her life in many respects, she was still somewhat shy when it came to making the first move. It just wasn't in her nature to be the instigator. She was surprised enough in herself that she had built a profile in the first place.

Just as she was getting ready to sign off, a little notice popped up indicating she had a new message. As the butterflies in her stomach flapped their wings, Jackie opened the message. She was relieved to find it wasn't another hoax.

His name was Adam, and he was forty years old. The picture displayed a casual, laid-back guy with a friendly smile. He liked hiking, reading, and watching minor-league baseball.

He had a ten-year-old son.

Jackie hadn't even considered the possibility that the man she dated would have children. She supposed it was likely, even, that a man her age would have been married before, and even if he hadn't been, they were certainly old enough to have fathered children. She found the thought exciting and intimidating at the same time. It would be amazing to become a mother, but a ten-year-old child would already be set in his ways. He would have his own personality, his own reservations. Perhaps he would resent her for dating his father.

Jackie leaned back in her chair. Adam seemed like a nice man. His message had been polite, complimentary, and funny. She would like to message him back. But she had to make sure she was okay with his son. How could she do that?

She found herself thinking about it all day: while whipping up a batch of chili at the soup kitchen, while participating in her baking class, while making dinner. It was unfair to disregard a man simply because he had a child, but if she was looking for a serious relationship – and she was – she had to look at the big picture. If they were to get married (the butterflies started up again at the thought), she would become a stepmother. And stepmothers did not have the best reputation. While she would like to think she would be understanding, and patient, and supportive, the child she would be parenting may not want her around.

Perhaps she was jumping the gun. The child could be perfectly respectful and accepting. He might want her around more than anything. Maybe he lost his mother and wants someone to fill that role. Without meeting him, or at least knowing more about him, she simply couldn't make an educated decision.

So she would message Adam back.

The conversation flowed back and forth a couple of times before they set a day and time to meet. It had been months since Jackie had been on a real date, but as of Friday night, that would no longer be the case. Jackie didn't know how to feel, but she was looking forward to it. At the very least, she reasoned, it would be excellent practice. The only social interaction she had had recently with a member of the opposite sex was her screwed up relationship with Paul. That didn't exactly set a good example for how her relationships should be.

Of course that brought up a whole other issue: how was she going to act? Her last "date" had been with a friend of a friend. They had a common connection, and while it hadn't been the most successful date, it hadn't been horrible. At least they had had something to talk about. Of course it helped that the gentleman – if she could even call him that – was a bit on the self-centered side and could probably carry on the conversation single-handedly. Jackie hadn't had to worry about being nervous; she could scarcely get a word in edgewise.

But now all she knew was what Adam had said in his messages and on his profile. There was no common connection, and Jackie hoped he wouldn't be as self-absorbed as Carl had been. So what would she talk about? They both enjoyed reading. Perhaps she could start with that. But what if they didn't like the same authors?

Jackie's heart started racing. Maybe she wasn't ready for this. Maybe she should message Adam back and cancel. Maybe she needed more time to feel comfortable in her own skin before she tried to start something new. Or maybe she just needed a little advice.

Jackie had met Mary's husband Bryan once before, when he had come to pick Mary up from book club when her car was in the shop. He had seemed like a nice guy. Maybe if she invited Mary and Bryan over for lunch they could help her prepare for her big date.

Jackie grabbed the phone before she could change her mind again.

Mary had barely gotten out a greeting before Jackie launched into her dilemma. Mary laughed.

"It's not funny," Jackie insisted.

"Oh, Jackie, it so is." And she laughed again. "Of course we'll help. I'm not exactly an expert in dating, but I'm sure Bryan can at least give you some pointers on conversing with men. Even just talking to him might help ease your fears."

"I hope so." Jackie was starting to sweat at this point. "I'm so nervous!"

"It's scary to put yourself out there," Mary acknowledged. "But I'm sure you'll be fine. You are a wonderful person, and any guy would be lucky to have you. If he doesn't agree, then he's not the guy for you."

"I know. And I've tried to tell myself that this could be practice at the very least. But it's still nerve-wracking."

"It'll be okay. Bryan and I will come over tomorrow, and hopefully we'll be able to talk you off this ledge. In the meantime try to take deep breaths and relax a little. You have almost a week to prepare."

"Thanks, Mary."

"Not a problem. So we'll see you tomorrow?"

"Yeah. Maybe noonish?"

"Sounds good."

"Okay. I'll see you then."

They said their good-byes, and Jackie clicked off the cordless handset. Now she just had to figure out what she was making for lunch.

Paul couldn't sleep. He couldn't eat. What had started as a hobby had quickly become an obsession. But it was the weekend, he reasoned. What else did he have to do?

When he was nearly doubled over in pain from hunger, he acknowledged he had to take a break. But he could eat in front of the computer, right? People did it all the time. So he made himself a sandwich and returned to the office.

He had long since broadened his horizons. Now, in addition to the forums with other medical professionals, he visited forums for thirty-somethings, for the newly divorced, and for those who lost a loved one. He couldn't stay on that last one for long; it was too depressing. But it was therapeutic to discuss the feelings of loneliness, abandonment, and vacancy that had been present since Uncle Bill died. It probably wouldn't have hit him so hard, he reasoned, if he wasn't living in Bill's house, working in Bill's office, sitting on Bill's desk chair. But he was, and he felt that void every day. So it helped to get the words out a little. At least others knew what he was going through.

It was the same in the newly-divorced forum. They knew how he felt. They understood what was going through his mind. Heck, they had even helped him comprehend his interactions with Jackie. He was projecting, they said. He wanted to be wanted, and he wanted to want. Jackie had been convenient. The fact that she was appealing made it all the easier. But it wasn't an excuse.

As for the thirty-somethings, well that just made him feel alive. He could talk about where he was in life, what he still wanted to do, to be. He could just chat, be himself.

Bouncing from one forum to another took more time than one would think. The hours slipped by, and before he knew it, the day had turned to night, then day again. He rubbed the stubble on his chin and squeezed his eyes shut. The glare of the computer monitor was taking its toll. Maybe just a few more minutes and he would call it quits.

An hour later Paul finally closed the laptop. His eyes were dry and tight, and he squeezed them shut. Rolling his neck, he stretched out the lower half of his body, then stood up.

It was a bright, sunny day outside. The light reflecting off week-old snow nearly blinded him. The snow would probably be gone by the following day, and something about that saddened him. Nature in winter was depressing without a crisp layer of white blanketing it. But he was used to depressing; he faced it every day.

Paul picked up the various snack packages that were scattered over the surface of the desk. He would definitely have to eat a healthy dinner to try to offset the damage he had done. But first, he had to get some sleep. It was already mid afternoon, and without sleep he wouldn't be able to function at the office in the morning. In his line of work, that simply wasn't acceptable.

Paul tossed the wrappers in the trash and dragged himself to bed. It didn't take long to fall asleep.

He woke up thirteen hours later.

He expected it to be dark when he woke. He figured it was about seven or eight o'clock. He was just about to pull himself out of bed when his alarm clock blared, startling him into falling backward. It couldn't possibly be five in the morning. But sure enough, the red numbers confirmed it. Apparently he had been more tired than he thought.

All while getting dressed Paul mused about how surreal a weekend it had been. The hours had flown by – something they hadn't done for months. And now he felt disoriented, unsure whether it was day or night, whether he was coming or going. He didn't like feeling out of control, but something about the weekend held its appeal. For the first time in a long time, he had felt alive. He had thrown caution to the wind, opened up to other people, been himself. While the aftermath was less than ideal, the reality had been invigorating. And his fingers itched to get back on the computer.

But it was Monday morning, and he had to get to work. He had patients to see. He couldn't live his life holed up in his office with a laptop. He had to get up, take a shower, and get ready for his day.

As he was backing his car down the driveway, Paul released a depressed breath. He was delivering gifts this week after work, starting today. For the first time he regretted volunteering to help. It was tempting to call and say he couldn't be there, after all. But he was a man of his word, and he wouldn't back out now. People were counting on him. His forum friends would just have to wait.

Chapter 24

Mondays were usually quiet for Jackie. The soup kitchen had extra volunteers, so she didn't go in. She didn't have any classes. Today she would be going to town hall to assist in the distribution of the holiday food and gift baskets, but that was only in the afternoon. An entire morning stretched ahead of her with nothing holding her back, and Jackie decided to take a few extra moments to enjoy the warmth of her bed.

Lunch the previous day had been successful. She had settled on warm, comforting pot roast for lunch, and Mary and Bryan had been very complimentary of the results. She didn't know how far she had gotten with easing her nerves for her date, but Bryan had given her some pointers, and Mary had reassured her that if she just acted like herself she would be fine. Having not gone on a date in a very long time, Jackie was still nervous. But she had enjoyed spending the day with friends.

Mary was definitely looking pregnant these days, though she was just over halfway there. Since her morning sickness had passed, she was able to enjoy the meal, and it was obvious she had relished it. "You don't know how much you enjoy something until it's taken away from you," she had commented with a laugh. "And I definitely enjoy eating!"

Bryan was a doting husband and father-to-be. He had watched Mary with a careful eye, making sure she didn't overdo it. There had been a minor scare a month or so ago when Mary had had some light bleeding, and they weren't taking any chances. For now she was just taking it easy, though there had been talk about her taking the rest of the school year off. Mary loved being a teacher, but being on her feet all day, keeping track of young children, definitely took its toll. She came home exhausted, and by the time the weekend rolled around, she had little energy for much of anything.

They had gotten close, Jackie mused. She and Mary. Jackie had never been one to make friends easily, but something about Mary had been comforting, welcoming. Jackie had noticed it the first couple of book club meetings that Mary had been a part of. And once Jackie started asking for Mary's advice about changing her life, the relationship had taken off. She was more comfortable with Mary than she had been with anyone else in a long time. She was grateful to have Mary in her life. She had to admit her life wouldn't be quite the same without her. Would she have had the courage to take charge? Would she have known where to start? Mary had been a sounding board, and Jackie had needed one badly.

Jackie stretched her arms over her head and turned to look at her clock radio. It was barely eight o'clock: a late wake-up time for the old Jackie, but still early for the floating-along Jackie. What would she do this morning?

Her volunteer work had been keeping her busy, especially when partnered with classes. She still had college applications to fill out, but there was still time before the deadlines. She had decided to pursue her Bachelor's of Social Work, and, though still nervous, she was excited about the possibilities. Of course that wouldn't start until the following fall, but it was something to look forward to.

She should probably spend some time looking for a paying job. While she loved what she was doing now – and thought she would love what she hoped to do in the future – neither was bringing in any income at the moment. And she couldn't afford to float forever, especially with upcoming college tuition bills to look forward to. Maybe she should check out the online job boards.

Then again, Christmas was a week and a half away, and she still had gifts to buy. A weekday morning was probably the best time to shop this time of year. With a nod, Jackie decided to spend the morning shopping. She hoisted herself out of bed and began running through her gift list while she got ready. There was her mother. And her father. Her younger brother, his wife, and their five-year-old daughters. She wanted to pick up something small for the full-timers at the soup kitchen, and perhaps baking supplies so she could whip up cookies for the part-timers and the people who dined there.

Christmas day should be interesting. She was helping at the soup kitchen around lunch time, then heading to her parents' house mid-afternoon. She hadn't told anyone about her life changes. She'd been fortunate that her mother hadn't inquired too much into what she'd been up to lately. But something was bound to come up during dinner, and Jackie wasn't comfortable lying to her family.

It *felt* like lying, not telling her mother what was going on. And she knew she wouldn't be able to keep it going forever. But for once she wanted to do what she wanted to do – without her mother butting her opinion in. Was that too much to ask? Was it too much to want to live her life the way she wanted to? No, she didn't have all the answers yet. She didn't have everything lined up. And she knew her mother would ask. Then there would be the disappointed silence. Jackie could picture her mother's look of disappointment with very little effort. She had seen it so often. Nothing was ever good enough.

Jackie often wondered what her life would be like if she had had the freedom to do whatever she wanted. If she had been able to pursue anything at college. If she could be part of different clubs in school, pursue different activities. Would she still be this subdued, reserved, timid woman? Or would she be more adventurous? Would she have thrown caution to the wind with Paul? Would she have quit her job years ago? Would she have ever even had that job? Would she have ever even met Paul?

Of course she would never know. But that didn't keep her from wondering. At least she had started making some decisions about what she was going to do with her life. Now if she only had a paying job, she would be good to go. But that was a worry for another day. Today, she was going shopping.

Jackie wasn't much of a shopper, at least not for herself. But she loved buying gifts for other people. There was just something about finding that perfect present for someone, and she looked forward to Christmas just so she could see her loved ones open their gifts.

Despite her better judgment, Jackie decided to go to the mall. There were specialty stores there that would have the perfect gift for her father: a difficult man to buy for, and a science buff. Plus, perhaps she could find something to go with the presents she had already bought for her nieces in Boston.

Thinking back to Boston, Jackie sighed. Life had felt so peaceful then, walking through the snow with Paul. Even with monumental decisions hanging over her, she had been happy, hopeful. She still was now, but it felt different. In Boston she had been young and carefree; In Munsen she had to be a grown-up. But, she supposed, you had to face the music eventually. She just had to be grateful to have had the experience at all.

The mall was busy, but not ridiculously crowded. Jackie was able to find a parking spot with relative ease, and the next two and a half hours flew by as she strolled from store to store. By the time she paused for lunch in the food court she had crossed her father, nieces and sister-in-law off her list. Perhaps tomorrow she would head to the grocery store to buy baking supplies. Not only did she have cookies to make, but she had also decided to whip up a couple of loaves of her famous strawberry nut bread – her brother's favorite – for Christmas dinner. That would be her project for the following weekend.

It was interesting watching people hustle around the mall. There were the college kids home on break, chatting with friends and laughing. There were the little kids with their parents, waiting in line to see Santa. There were the individual women power-walking through the stores, obviously stressed and tight on time.

And then there was Jackie, sitting by herself, shopping for people she saw a couple of times a year, for the most part alone in the world. It was easy to get sucked into a self-pitying state. She had to remind herself that she had friends, and coworkers and classmates and people who relied on her. She wasn't alone, not really.

But it sure felt like it sometimes.

She wondered how the date would go on Friday. She didn't want to put too much stock in it, but she was anxious to be in a relationship. She was tired of floating through life by herself, going home to an empty house, eating alone, sleeping alone. While she was comfortable with her own company, it got lonely. And times like this, when she saw families and friends spending time together, were the hardest. Add the holidays to that, and it was even worse.

Jackie shook her head. She had to get herself out of this mood. This afternoon she had to smile and be full of holiday cheer. She had, after all, decided to go with Paul to deliver gifts. She could use the companionship, and she needed to put things into perspective. Her life could be a lot worse. She could be struggling with having a roof over her head and food in her belly. Though, she supposed, that might be her if she didn't get a real job one of these days. But that was far down the line. She still had money. She should still be grateful. And she needed to reinforce that to herself.

Crumpling up her napkin, Jackie gathered up her garbage and picked up her shopping bags. It was time to get home. She had to drop off her purchases before heading to the town hall. And there were gifts to gather up before hitting the road with Paul.

She really hoped the offer still stood. She hadn't exactly been nice about it. She had to find a way to smooth things over. Mary was right; there was something unresolved there. That was one of the reasons she had decided to just go for it. Before things had gotten awkward, they had been doing well. There had been the stirrings of a great friendship, and it would be a shame to throw that away.

She was ready and waiting for him when he arrived. She had gathered up the day's deliveries. They just needed to load up and go.

Paul looked terrible. His eyes were bloodshot; his face was drawn. He looked like he was either seriously ill or had just received some really bad news.

"Are you okay?" It was the first thing that came out of Jackie's mouth. Perhaps not the best greeting, but she was worried about him.

Paul nodded. "Yeah, I'm fine. Just had a long weekend."

Jackie paused before saying "okay." After a moment of awkward silence, she continued. "I was hoping you were still willing to let me tag along today."

"You want to come with me?"

Jackie nodded. "If you'll let me."

She wasn't surprised by his hesitation.

"I know I said some things last week that I probably shouldn't have. I'm sorry. I didn't mean to offend you. Things just came out a little more harshly than I intended."

"It's okay. I wasn't offended. Surprised, yes. Offended, no. You seemed to have made up your mind about things, and I had to respect that. Why the change of heart?"

Jackie shrugged. "It's hard to explain. I guess I just have this feeling that things are still unsettled with us. We were starting to be friends – good friends, I think – then things got all messed up. And we haven't really had any resolution to anything. I guess I want to give our friendship a chance and see what happens." She paused a moment, and she could see Paul processing. "Plus, I really want to see the expressions on people's faces when they see what we bring them," she added with a smile.

Paul smiled briefly back, but he took another moment before saying "you can come along."

Jackie took a deep breath. "Great. I've gathered all the gifts and food baskets together. We just have to load them into the van."

"Okay. I'll get the keys from the office and pull it around to the front of the building."

"I'll start moving things to the front door."

He nodded, and Jackie watched him go. After his indication last week that he had wanted to be friendly, his standoffishness was throwing her off. Then again, maybe he was still reluctant to accept her at her word. She certainly wouldn't blame him. Her feelings on the subject had been all over the spectrum, and she hadn't been shy about sharing them. She wouldn't blame him if he decided he wanted nothing to do with her after all. She hoped he would give her a shot, but if not, then at least she would know that things were over. That would be the end, and she wouldn't push the issue if it came to that. She could only hope that this time together would start getting them back on more secure footing – and maybe pick up where the road trip had left off. Perhaps it was fitting that this new beginning would be starting off on the road. It would be a mini road trip to salvage the memory of their attempt at a real one.

As with their first voyage, tension and silence filled the vehicle. She found it strange to be sitting here with Paul – knowing him, and yet not knowing him. Being familiar with who he was just a few short weeks ago, but being nearly a stranger with who he had become. She didn't know how to talk to him, and she couldn't read him to determine if he even wanted her to talk to him. Perhaps it would be best if they just started fresh.

"So what have you been up to, Paul?"

He shrugged. "Not much. Work, home. Since the holiday fair was last weekend, I've been a little lost. I haven't known what to do with myself. Everything's pretty much shut down for the holidays."

"It tends to do that."

"Yeah."

Jackie relaxed back in her seat, relieved that she had been able to draw Paul into conversation, however brief. She didn't even mind the silence that fell afterward. At least it felt companionable instead of forced.

Paul wished he had backed out of volunteering. He had finally been coming to terms with his feelings toward Jackie, and now she was pushing herself back into his life. It was his own darn fault, but he figured after their conversation the previous week he didn't have to worry about it anymore. Her tagging along to deliver gifts had thrown him off. But should he tell her he had changed his mind? That he wanted a clean split? Was that even what he wanted? Or had he just wanted an explanation, an understanding of his feelings?

By the time they pulled up to the first home, he was grateful for the distraction. Really, he reasoned, he should be thankful that he was the one delivering gifts, not receiving them. His biggest problems were figuring out Jackie and finding time to go online to check in on his forums. He didn't have to worry about a roof over his head or food in his belly. Why couldn't he just count his blessings for once?

He and Jackie exited the van, gathered up the food basket and assorted gift bags, and walked up the front pathway. The door opened before they even rang the bell, and the woman who answered had tears in her eyes.

"Happy holidays!" Jackie greeted with a smile.

The woman beckoned them in without a word. From the entryway Paul could see a meager Christmas tree in a corner of the living room, decorated with handmade ornaments and strands of popcorn. It was quaint and old-fashioned, and he found himself thinking that even if they didn't have money, these people had creativity, faith, and joy. These days, who could take the time to make their own decorations? It was all store-bought ornaments shining above piles of gifts, most of which would be forgotten in a couple of weeks. Paul was sure the few presents under this tree had been carefully selected, thoughtfully wrapped, and would be treasured for much longer.

He turned from the quaint scene to find Jackie chatting with the woman. She had a way about her, Jackie did. She could put almost anyone at ease. It had served her well in a pediatrician's office, and he was sure it helped in her numerous volunteer positions, as well. She was so honest, so genuine, that people couldn't help but open up to her. Take this woman for instance. She was talking about how her husband was on disability, and that they couldn't afford to buy their children expensive gifts. But they were good kids, she insisted, and they deserved so much more.

By the time they left, Paul's heart had gone out to this family, and he was grateful Jackie had come along. He would have felt awkward, unsure of what to say or how to act. Jackie had eased the tension, made everyone comfortable, as if they were old friends getting together for a chat. He couldn't help but express his gratitude when they got in the car.

"Thanks, Jackie."

She looked up from securing her seat belt, surprise in her eyes. "For what?"

"For making this so easy. I wouldn't have known what to say to her. I probably would have just shoved the bags in her face and walked out."

Jackie laughed. "You would not have. They're just people, Paul. There's no reason to feel awkward. They're really no different than you and me."

"Rationally I know that. Emotionally, though…I don't know. I guess it just strikes a chord."

"It's okay."

"I guess I'm glad you tagged along after all."

"Me, too." She flashed a smile at him then turned her attention to the paperwork on her lap. "Looks like our next stop is about a mile and a half from here."

Halfway through the day, he started to realize that his feelings for Jackie weren't just a need to want somebody. There was something special about her. By the end of the day, he had nearly convinced himself he was in love with her.

What was it about being on the road with this woman? Was it the confined space? The having no one else to talk to?

He needed to process this. He needed to figure out what the hell was going on. How could he be thinking about pushing her out of his life one minute and pulling her into his arms the next? What was wrong with him?

He bid Jackie farewell, with the understanding that when he went out to deliver gifts on Thursday that she would be joining him again. But could he really take another day with her? He was already going crazy. Not that he could blame her for that one – he was the one who didn't even know how he felt.

The more he thought about it, though, the more he wondered if Jackie might be having the same issue. Hadn't she gone back and forth on how their relationship – or lack thereof – should proceed? Hadn't she kept changing her mind about if she wanted to be his friend or wanted nothing to do with him? Maybe she was just as confused as he was. Who knew? Maybe she even had feelings for him but was trying to suppress them, as he was.

By the time he got home he was thoroughly disgusted with himself and tired of turning the problem over and over in his mind. He tossed his keys on the table by the entryway, went to the office to turn on the computer, then swung by the kitchen to grab a bite to eat. The way he was feeling, he didn't know if it would be better to log on to the divorced singles forum or the thirty-somethings forum. Did he want to hash out his feelings or escape them? Probably both. He would probably end up going back and forth for a bit.

Popping a frozen meal into the microwave, he thought about Jackie. This really had to stop. He was getting obsessed. Who knew he had such an addictive personality? First the forums, now Jackie. What was next? The casinos? Alcohol?

Paul rubbed a hand down his face. He was slowly losing his mind. Maybe it was the lack of sleep. Or the boredom. Or just the inability to grasp what it was he really wanted.

When the microwave dinged, he decided to forego the computer a bit and zone out to the TV instead. He brought the meal to the living room and rested it on a tray table his uncle had conveniently placed beside the sofa. He wondered how many nights were spent doing just this: waiting for the time to tick by while consuming a nutritionally-questionable meal in front of the tube. Did his uncle feel this way? Was he bored, restless? It hadn't seemed so to Paul, but, really, how much time had he spent with his uncle? Before the separation, they saw each other primarily on special occasions: Christmas, Easter, the occasional wedding, funeral or graduation. Then he was always busy socializing, catching up with people he saw a couple of times a year. There was no time to be restless and bored. And he had always seemed so jovial, so friendly and upbeat. Was it all a façade?

Grateful for the shift in his thoughts away from Jackie, Paul pondered a bit. It was sad to think about Uncle Bill alone in this big house, lonely and depressed. He had no children to visit him, not even a pet to distract him. Paul hadn't had the time to swing by, and he doubted many other relatives did, either. Bill had been all alone.

He supposed there must have been friends. Perhaps he and Jackie had socialized out of work. Or maybe there were others. He had obviously been popular – his funeral had been crowded with people paying their respects. Maybe he had been part of clubs or organizations in town. The senior center was popular, he understood. And there were always activities going on. Maybe, like Paul, he had sought extracurricular tasks to keep him occupied. Maybe these nights in front of the TV were few and far between.

Then again, maybe they weren't.

Paul ended up falling asleep in front of the television, a half-eaten TV dinner left on the table. He woke up around midnight to find infomercials blaring on the screen and a faint rumbling stirring his belly. He flicked off the set and stood up, stretching.

After swinging by the kitchen to dispose of his dinner remains and pick up a snack, he shuffled down the hall toward his bedroom. En route he paused in front of the office. He never had made it online. Instead he had wallowed in memories of a man he barely knew.

"I'm not like Uncle Bill," he told himself. "I have friends, and coworkers, and projects to keep me busy. I will not be lonely. I will not be bored. My life is my own." With that, he completed his trek down the hallway and got ready for bed.

Jackie went to bed feeling content. While she enjoyed her volunteer work, she didn't often get the opportunity to interact with people on a one-on-one basis. It had been nice to socialize and get to know the people she was helping. And the time with Paul had been nice, too. She was looking forward to Thursday. Though it held its own appeal, it should also help her keep her mind off of Friday – and her impending date. She was hoping delivering gifts and spending time with Paul would be a sufficient distraction. Maybe if she kept herself busy some of the fear would dissipate. One could hope, anyway.

Somewhere around the middle of their deliveries, the tension had eased between her and Paul. They had seemed to stand on more secure footing again. It had been a relief. She still didn't know how she felt or what she wanted, but it was nice to know they could at least get along again. It had felt wrong, somehow, to be at such odds with him. Though they didn't owe each other anything, it kind of felt like they did. There was a link there, a bond, that she hadn't felt right throwing away. Maybe that was why she had been struggling so hard with coming to a decision and sticking to it. Her brain was telling her it was best to cut ties, but her heart and gut were telling her otherwise. She felt more at peace now, as if a missing puzzle piece was now securely in place, as if a weight had lifted off her shoulders. Now she could focus on moving forward in her life, instead of dwelling on the past.

Chapter 25

The phone rang early the next morning. Surprised, Jackie reached for the receiver by her bed.

"So it's true."

Her mother's voice caused Jackie to sit up abruptly.

"Hi, Mom."

There was no greeting. "What are you doing home on a Tuesday morning? Don't you have to go to work?"

She didn't want to lie to her mother, but she didn't want to ask for an argument, either. "I'm going in later." Technically, it was true. She had lunch shift at the soup kitchen.

"Are you sick?"

"No."

Silence fell. After a moment, her mother asked "that's it?"

Jackie sighed. "There have been some changes in my life recently. I don't really have time to get into them right now. I'll talk to you about them at Christmas."

"Did you lose your job?"

Obviously her mother wasn't going to drop the subject. "No. I left voluntarily."

"You left? To do what?"

How could she answer that? Anything that wasn't a lie would just disappoint. "To find myself."

Jackie could practically hear the eye roll. "Oh, for crying out loud. You don't know where you are? I can tell you."

"It's complicated, Mom. I'll talk to you at Christmas."

"I expect answers."

"You'll get them. I promise. I have to go."

After a hurried good-bye, Jackie hung up the phone. Her breath was heavy. Who would have known she was home? Who would have known and told her mother she was home? She had hoped to be more prepared before confronting her mother. She had at least hoped to have some kind of explanation that wouldn't send her mother off the deep end. She doubted her mother would be able to wait until Christmas. Now she would have to start screening her calls. Great.

Jackie dragged herself out of bed and shuffled into the kitchen. After taking a moment to make a cup of tea, she fell into a chair at the kitchen table. Okay, so her mother knew she wasn't working at the doctor's office anymore. No problem. She was going to find out eventually. Now Jackie just needed to find an acceptable reason for leaving without having another job lined up, volunteering when she should be working, looking at colleges when she already had a degree, and still being single at her age. That last one had nothing to do with her employment, but it was bound to come up at some point. After all, in her mother's eyes, if she was married with children, this whole situation would never have happened. Her life would be complete and happy, and she wouldn't have a single care. Yeah, right. Suffice it to say she and her mother had different expectations and ideas of what life should be. Not that Jackie didn't want to be married with children – she did – but it wasn't the be all and end all. She was still a person. She was still an individual. And she still had needs and wants that went farther than starting a family. Especially when that family was nowhere to be found.

If she had a boyfriend to bring home, that would distract her mother enough to get her off Jackie's case for a bit. But Jackie certainly didn't expect her date on Friday to go *that* well. And even if it did go well, she couldn't very well ask him to go with her to Christmas dinner. That would scare him off more quickly than anything else she could think to say. Maybe Paul would be willing...No. Jackie dismissed that with a firm shake of her head. They were just starting to get on more secure footing again. She didn't want to go and mess things up again.

No, she had to acknowledge that there would be no distractions. She had to come armed with the truth – or at least a version of the truth that would satisfy her mother. That meant a job, security, and prospects. How on earth would she come up with all that in a week?

Paul's head was pounding when he forced himself to open his eyes. He felt like he'd been hit by a bus. Or at least had enough to drink that he would have fallen down a flight of stairs. He had overslept, but it was still barely light out. Would he be able to get to the office on time?

He felt like he had when Pam had first kicked him out. It was a struggle to get out of bed. He hadn't expected the evening's musings to affect him so much, but he had spent a lot of the night tossing and turning, enveloped in disturbing dreams about Uncle Bill being sad and alone, Jackie telling him she was running off with this guy she was seeing, Pam telling him she was getting remarried. And through it all he had been left feeling helpless, deserted, and inadequate. It had been a rough night.

But he couldn't disappoint his patients. That had been one of the cons he had come up with when determining if he should take over the practice: if he was sick or not feeling well, he couldn't as easily take a day off. In a group practice, others could help with some of his calls. By himself, they would all need to be rescheduled. Sure, there were other offices he had arrangements with in cases of emergency, but he didn't want to call in a favor already. He had barely been in business two months. So he dragged himself to the office and struggled through the day. He could only hope that his patients couldn't tell how he was feeling, or what he was thinking. All he wanted to do was go home and curl up in bed.

By the time he got home, however, he had gotten a second wind. Then he was bored, restless, wandering from room to room, ghosts of his past haunting him. He had to get out, do something. It was a shame he had to wait until tomorrow to deliver gifts again with Jackie. But maybe he should go out and buy some gifts himself. He still hadn't picked up anything for his mother and stepfather. He had planned on purchasing something when he was at the holiday fair, but he had been so wrapped up in the logistics that he hadn't had much of a chance to really look around. It was a shame; there seemed to be some really nice stuff there. Now he would have to settle for generic shopping mall trinkets.

He grabbed his coat and keys before he could talk himself out of a shopping mall at Christmastime. He needed a distraction. He wasn't really one for shopping to begin with. Add crowds of people to the mix, and he expected the excursion would be less than pleasant. But it had to happen sometime, and he figured a weeknight had to be better than the weekend.

He spent two hours wandering the stores, finally settling on a pair of earrings for his mother and a briefcase for his stepfather. He wondered if he should buy something for Pam. He had never not bought her anything before. But would that be too personal? Would it be seen as an attempt to rekindle a relationship? He went back and forth for a bit before settling on a card. He would send her a card, write a nice note in it, and be done.

What about Jackie? The question popped into his head before he could stop it. Well, what about her? Their friendship was tenuous at best. There was certainly no expectation of a gift from her. He didn't think she would expect one of him. But suddenly he wanted to give her something. Something related to cooking occurred to him, but he didn't know how that would be received. She had decided not to pursue it as a career, and he wanted her to know he had been listening to her. But what did someone get a person who was going into social work? It wasn't exactly a gift-giving occupation.

He was passing a bookstore when the idea came to him. And as he picked up and paid for the leather datebook, he smiled for the first time that day.

It wasn't a great day to deliver presents, Jackie had to admit. But they had an obligation to their clientele, and Jackie wouldn't let a little slush and cold stand in her way. She was ready and waiting when Paul pulled into the town hall parking lot.

"Lots to deliver today," she greeted him with a smile.

"Glad to hear it."

He seemed in better spirits today, more laid-back. She was glad he would be starting up as they had left off. She would take it as a good omen.

The next few hours flew by. They were well-received by everyone, and with each home they visited, Jackie's sureness in her new chosen profession grew. This was what she was about: helping people, showing them others cared. If she could positively affect even one life, she would consider herself successful.

As they pulled back into the parking lot, Jackie turned to Paul. "Thanks for helping out today. I had a good time."

"Me, too. Hey, before you leave, I have something in my car for you."

"For me?"

"Yeah." He parked the van, and together they entered the town hall. Jackie waited while Paul slid the van's keys into the slot on the door for the social services office. What could he possibly have for her? Had she left something behind at the office, or during their road trip?

They walked back to the parking lot in silence. When they reached Paul's car, he pulled out a small wrapped package and handed it to her. "Merry Christmas."

"A present?" She stared at him with a dropped jaw. "But I didn't get you anything."

He shrugged. "It's okay. It's nothing much. I just saw it and thought of you."

"Do you want me to open it now?"

"If you'd like."

Jackie loved presents. She knew she should probably wait until Christmas, but she couldn't resist.

"Oh, Paul, it's lovely."

"I'm glad you like it." He paused for a moment while she examined the datebook, then he reached for her hand. "I have an idea."

She turned to meet his gaze with quizzical eyes. "Okay."

"We both know that you and I have had our ups and downs. Our relationship has had more twists and turns than most relationships lasting years longer."

Jackie laughed. "You could say that."

"So here's what I propose. I still have loose ends. You still have loose ends. We both still have things to figure out. I propose we step back, figure out what we're doing with our lives, then meet up six months from now and start over. No weirdness, no he said/she said, he did/she did. We'll just see what happens."

Jackie thought about it for a moment. They had definitely had their ups and downs. And they had definitely had their awkwardness. Yet she valued him as a friend. Perhaps it would be best to start over, clean slate. Then they could stand on more secure footing again.

"I think I'd like that."

He released a breath. "I was hoping you'd say that. Turn to June 18."

Jackie flipped open the planner to the designated date and laughed. In red pen Paul had written "COFFEE WITH PAUL."

"Good thing I didn't say 'no.'"

"I didn't think you would. I was hoping you wouldn't, anyway."

"So it looks like we'll be getting together on June 18."

"If that's all right with you."

"It's fine." She paused. "And I guess that means we won't be seeing each other until then?"

Paul hesitated. "I admit it was the weakest part of my plan. But I think it might be for the best. That way we can really figure out what we want without the drama holding us back."

Jackie took a deep breath. "Okay."

"Thank you for your help delivering presents."

"Thank you for allowing me. I had a good time."

"Me, too. I hope you have a merry Christmas, and a happy new year."

"You, too, Paul."

They hugged then, and though there was some awkwardness, Jackie felt Paul's fondness for her as well. He kissed her cheek as they pulled away, squeezed her hand, then moved to the driver's seat door of his car.

"Take care of yourself. I want you to make it to June 18 in one piece."

"I'll do my best."

They bid each other farewell, and Paul drove off. Jackie watched him go, unsure if she should be sad or not. For all their ups and downs, she would miss him.

She wondered what the coming months would bring, and how they would both change.

Jackie stuffed her hands in her pockets and walked the short distance to her car. As she waited for the engine to warm up, her thoughts returned to her mother. She had a lot to figure out in the next six months. Heck, she had a lot to figure out in the next week. But if there was one benefit to the drama, it was that she had nearly forgotten about her date the following evening – and the nerves that had been possessing her since she had set it up. Perhaps there was hope for her yet.

Chapter 26

The nerves came back fast and furious as Jackie was picking out an outfit for the date. She went back and forth, trying to decide if she had nothing appropriate to wear or if she should just wear her normal clothes – and that if he didn't like them, then he wouldn't like her. She ended up digging out a years-old dress that flattered her but was a bit too formal for regular wear. She didn't know the dress code for where they were going for dinner, and she would rather be overdressed than underdressed.

It was strange, she mused a half hour later as she got into her car, to be meeting her date at the restaurant. Though she agreed it was safer and more practical, she was an old-fashioned girl at heart, and always pictured a date picking her up at home. Were these strange feelings a bad omen for the evening ahead? Or was she just being silly?

She was just being silly, she decided, when she spotted her date just fifteen minutes later. He was attractive, looked friendly, and his profile appeared to be accurate. She greeted him shyly, introduced herself, and sat across from him while he stood politely.

Despite initial nerves, the conversation flowed smoothly. There were plenty of topics on which they agreed or could at least have a friendly debate, and Jackie found herself relaxing. Over dessert she decided to approach the subject that gave her the greatest pause.

"So tell me about your son."

Adam grinned. "He's awesome."

Jackie laughed. "I'm glad you think so. What's he like?"

"Oh, I suppose he's your typical ten-year-old boy. He loves his video games. Fortunately, though, he also loves his soccer. He stays pretty active."

"Do you get a chance to see him play?"

Adam nodded. "All the time. The custody arrangement with my ex-wife means I have him every weekend and most holidays, so I take him to most of his games. He's pretty good. I'm impressed. He definitely doesn't get it from me!"

"He must be looking forward to Christmas."

"Absolutely. His list to Santa is a mile long."

"I'm sure. It must be so much fun to watch him open his presents."

"It can be. I don't get the full effect, though. I get him Christmas Eve, but Christmas day is the one holiday I don't get to keep him. He actually spends the Christmas Eve day with me, then goes back to Mom's after the festivities at his grandparents' house."

"So no Santa?"

"Not with me." Adam shrugged. "I wish I could be with him, but it was really important to Nicole to have him that day, so I agreed to it. She's been more into Christmas than I have, so I can't complain too much."

"At least you get him Christmas Eve."

"Absolutely. We go to my parents' house and open presents. He gets completely spoiled, then goes back to Mom with a sugar high." Adam laughed. "I guess that's my little revenge. I imagine it's hard to get him to bed after all the excitement."

"But if he wants Santa to come..." Jackie smiled.

"Yeah." He took a sip of his coffee and leaned back in his chair.

"So what do you do on Christmas day?"

"Not much. Watch TV in my boxers." He grinned. "It's a quiet day. I catch up on things around the house. How about you?"

"I go to my parents' house." She made a face, and Adam laughed.

"Not a fan?"

Jackie sighed. "I love my parents, really I do. But my mother seems to have this picture in her head of what my life should be like, and I am sadly lacking."

"Your life doesn't seem to be lacking from what I can tell. You seem pretty happy with your volunteer work and plans for the future."

She nodded. "I am. But that won't be enough for her. She wants me to be married, with kids, being a happy little homemaker. If not that, then in a job where I'll meet plenty of eligible men. I don't think the homeless guys I meet are her idea of eligible."

"No, I suppose not." He stared down into his coffee for a moment. "Personally, I kind of miss the family Christmas. As frustrating as they can be, parents mean well, and it's nice to just be able to enjoy their company."

"I know you're right. It's just difficult sometimes." She took a bite of her cheesecake. "Hey, you could always tag along, act as my buffer and get a dose of family." The moment she said it, she wished she could take it back. It had been so comfortable, talking to him like this, but she barely knew the man! "I'm sorry. That was presumptuous of me."

He waved away her concerns. "No, don't worry about it. I understand. Sitting here, chatting with you, it's hard to believe we've only just met."

"Strange, huh? And I was so nervous about this date."

"Not that I knew you before, but based on what you've said, it's probably because you're comfortable in your skin now. I gather you were a bit timid before."

Jackie nodded. "I was. In some ways I still am. But I've definitely made some pretty major strides. I feel more confident now, in my decisions and life choices. I think I'm heading in the right direction."

"It shows."

They sat in comfortable silence for a moment until the waiter brought their bill. As Adam reached for the bifold, he asked, "So was the invitation to join you on Christmas day a real one, or one that is best ignored?"

Jackie looked at him in surprise. "You want to spend the day with my family? With strangers?"

Adam shrugged. "It's better than sitting home alone, missing my son." He looked up at her and flashed her a grin. "And maybe I can help you with your mother."

Jackie gaped at him for a moment. Had she been serious in her invitation? A part of her hadn't wanted to show up at Christmas dinner alone, but was this seedling of a relationship the way to go? What if he did or said something inappropriate? She had no way of knowing if he was trustworthy. Perhaps he was really a criminal, looking for an opportunity to sneak into unsuspecting families' homes. He seemed honest and straightforward, but who could say?

After a moment's consideration, she suggested "why don't we hang out again and see how it goes?"

"A cautious woman, but sensible. I think that sounds like a great idea." He smiled at her again and tossed a few bills in the black folder.

Distracted by the movement, Jackie jumped. "Oh! I need to pay my way." She reached for her purse.

"Nonsense. It's my treat. This is a date after all."

"But that's not fair to you."

"I insist."

Jackie let her shoulders sag. "Okay. But can we make next time my treat?"

"You have a problem with a man paying for dates?"

"Not a problem. It just never seemed fair to me."

"You are a modern woman, Jackie. I think you're more independent than you gave yourself credit for."

Jackie blushed and shrugged. "I just view it as a question of fairness. Why should the guy pay when I bring in a salary as well?"

"You'd be surprised how many people disagree with you."

He walked her to her car, bid her farewell with a peck on the cheek, and proceeded to his own vehicle. As Jackie drove home, she reflected on how well the evening had gone. And how now she might even have a date for Christmas dinner.

Chapter 27

MAY

As Paul drove home from the office, he was looking forward to a quiet evening by himself. He had been quite a busy bee lately, with an influx of patients at the office and his meetings with the Economic Development Commission. He had also been participating in events held by the Chamber of Commerce, which had led to more social contacts and networking opportunities. A quiet evening at home was now a thing to be relished instead of dreaded.

He was glad the rain had finally let up. Maybe this week's farmer's market wouldn't be a washout. One could hope, anyway. After the success of his holiday fair, he would hate for the second event he ran to be a dud.

After tossing his keys on the table in the front entryway, Paul swung by the kitchen to grab a snack, then headed for the office. He still went on the forums these days, but usually just to check in and chat for a bit. His latest addiction was Facebook, where he was able to catch up with old college buddies and new acquaintances. He and Pam had even connected online, now that their relationship was on steadier footing. The divorce had been finalized in March, and, though things had been awkward in the beginning, he now considered her a friend. The history he had been so reluctant to give up was still there – but it could now be used as an asset in their friendship instead of a manipulation tool that caused him guilt. They got together once in a while for coffee, though it had been a couple of weeks since they had done so. Perhaps he should shoot her a message to see if she wanted to get together this weekend.

He wondered, sometimes, what Jackie was up to. He had looked her up online once, but he couldn't find a profile for her. She was probably too busy to be goofing off online, what with her volunteer work and classes and such. He looked forward to the following month, when he would be able to touch base with her again and see how she was doing. Until then he would have to be content with his musings.

He checked his e-mail quickly, logged on to Facebook for a bit, and killed a bit of time playing a game. After a few minutes, though, he found himself bored. He had been looking forward to not having plans, but he had grown too accustomed to being on the go. It would take more than a few minutes online to help him wind down. Hoping the fresh air would help, he decided to meander into the backyard.

This was definitely his favorite part of the house. Many a time the view had soothed his senses, relieved his stress, and calmed his mind. He could breathe more easily, think more clearly, and just appreciate life a little more.

The appreciating thing was getting easier, though. He was actually starting to like his life again. The practice was doing well, he was keeping busy, and he felt like he was actually utilizing his skill set. It was a good feeling. Now all he needed was a good woman by his side, and he would be set.

Coming to terms with Pam and their new relationship had gone a long way toward helping him in that respect. Rather than pine over what could have been, he was able to accept what had been. Yes, he missed Pam, but they were still a part of each other's lives. And he had to admit they were better friends than lovers. They meshed better. Emotions weren't so strained.

He had gone on a few dates to test the waters, see what was out there. He had met some nice women, but he hadn't yet found it – that magic spark that meant something special was happening. The closest he had gotten was Jackie, and he didn't want to start dwelling on that again. When they met up in June he would see how they felt. For all he knew she could be dating someone seriously. They could be talking marriage and kids. He could be moving into her cute little house.

The pain in his gut threw him off. He didn't want to think about Jackie with someone else. He wanted her to be happy, yes, but not with someone else. So did that mean he wanted her to be with him? Was he ready for the whole marriage thing again? Kids? Because that's what being with Jackie would mean. She wanted it all – and she deserved it. She should have the life she wanted. And if Paul wanted to be with her – not saying that he did, but *if* he did – than he would have to want it, too. So did he?

He dropped himself into an Adirondack chair and rested his head on his hands. He had thought it would be so simple. If he and Jackie clicked when they met up again, then they could proceed from there. But was he ready to open up that can of worms? If Jackie wanted to be with him, was he ready to be with her?

The past several months, working with the children at work, Paul had accepted the fact that he would like to be a father. He had also accepted the fact that it might not happen. He didn't think he could handle being a single dad, and the marriage thing kind of scared him. He had been down that road before, and he didn't know if he could take that chance again. He didn't know if he was ready to put his happiness in someone else's hands again.

Would he ever be? That was the real question. It wasn't like he was expecting to meet up with Jackie on the eighteenth and marry her on the nineteenth. It didn't work like that. But he had to think there was a reasonable chance of it happening eventually. He wouldn't drag Jackie along like that.

Paul looked at the empty Adirondack chair next to him. What would it be like to have someone sitting there? Someone who would always be there? Someone to hold at night, to eat dinner with, to share things with. While he had gotten used to his own company, that didn't mean he wouldn't welcome sharing it with someone else. He could picture Jackie there. He could picture laughing with her, talking with her, holding hands with her. Maybe he couldn't picture some random woman with him, but he could picture her. He wanted her to be part of his life.

Of course if there was no "spark," no chemistry, well, he would have to look elsewhere for love and accept that they were meant to be just friends. But if his breath caught at the sight of her – as it was doing now just thinking of her – well, maybe there was something there.

Would she feel the same? It was a big gamble, putting your heart out like that. He wished there was a way for him to test the waters. He wanted to know she wasn't attached, that she wasn't interested in someone else. Was there a way to do that?

She had mentioned something, back when they were delivering holiday gifts. She had had a date with some guy she had met online. They had met through an online dating site. What was the name? What was the name? It stood to reason that if she met one guy on there, she would probably have an account so she could meet others there as well. Maybe if her account was still active, he would know she wasn't seeing someone. Maybe he could contact her. You know, secretly. Without telling her it was him. Maybe he could get to know her. And she could get to know him – without the awkwardness that had invaded when he made the stupid mistake of kissing her. If she grew to like him for him – not their strange history, but who he really was – perhaps then he would know if they could have a future.

Perhaps it was time for him to make an online dating profile.

Jackie kicked the door closed with one foot before making her way into the kitchen. After placing the two over-sized bags of groceries on the table, she finally released a pent-up sigh. She was exhausted. Ever since she had taken over the office duties at the soup kitchen, she had been spending countless hours there. Unfortunately, she only managed a couple of hours working directly with their clientele. Fortunately, she was now getting paid, which meant she could keep doing what she enjoyed and put aside a little money for college. While financial aid would help a bit, she couldn't count on it to cover everything. Which meant she still had to come up with the rest. She was lucky that a paid position had become available at the kitchen; she hadn't been having much luck elsewhere. In retrospect, it may have been a mistake to leave her job in this economy without having something else lined up. But it all worked out. Her bills were getting paid, and she hadn't had to sacrifice her volunteering or her future plans.

In all realities, she was enjoying her work in the office. The books had been a mess when she began, and whipping everything into shape had proved a challenge. But Jackie found she enjoyed the organizing, problem-solving and planning. And when she did leave, she would definitely be leaving the office in much better shape. Though it may be some time before that happened. She didn't plan on looking for a permanent position until she got her degree, which meant she would need to stay employed until then. And working at a soup kitchen would look great on her resume. Since she was hoping to work with people in need, the soup kitchen would be great experience, as would the volunteer work she continued to do with the office of human services at the town hall.

Yes, she was definitely keeping busy these days. Though she had opted not to take any continuing education courses this spring, she had had no problem filling her hours. For a while, she had been spending time with Adam – going to movies, concerts, museums and the like. But they had parted ways back in April. While they got along fine, something had been missing. There hadn't been any chemistry. Time with him was simply time spent with a friend. Their kisses had been modest, their embraces warm. They still saw each once in a while, but they both knew they were destined to be friends and nothing more. Jackie's only regret had been his son, whom she had truly come to love. Spending time with Matt had made her long for a child of her own even more.

Which brought her to this evening's activities. Once the groceries were put away, she would be logging online to see if there had been any interest in her dating profile. She had reactivated it the previous week in the hope that something might come of it. So far she hadn't had much luck. But she wasn't in a hurry, not really. She would rather wait a bit and wind up with someone she could spend her life with than rush things and end up with someone unsuitable.

Jackie paused for a moment, her hand clutching a box of pasta. Was this really her, putting herself out there to meet men online? A year ago she wouldn't have thought it possible. She had kept to herself, quiet and shy, seemingly content to float along in her meaningless little life. Now here she was, taking charge. A new job, new experiences on the horizon, a new outlook on life. It felt good to be turning things around. And to think she had been scared to get started! Perhaps change wasn't so bad, after all.

A few minutes later Jackie was seated at her kitchen table, laptop open in front of her. She had a few new messages, but they were likely junk. She usually got a couple of messages from South African princes and the like, looking to meet "someone nice" from the States. She deleted three in rapid succession. One message, however, sounded promising. No picture, which always made her a little nervous, but he seemed like a nice guy. His name was Andrew, and his message was brief but polite. Perhaps it wouldn't hurt to reply.

It always gave her a little thrill to contact someone like this. At the same time, her nerves kicked up, sending her into a whirlwind of emotion that she couldn't decide if she liked or hated. To think: this could be her soul mate. Or, this could be a psycho. It was pretty much a crap shoot. But if she focused on the potential positive side, she would be much happier. So she would keep an open mind. And hope that Andrew messaged her back – without turning into a psycho.

Chapter 28

Paul decided to go with his middle name. He didn't want it to be too much of a lie. But at the same time he figured she'd quickly learn who he was if he gave his real name. He didn't like deceiving her, but he didn't know how else to get to know her without jeopardizing things. Besides, he had a feeling this would be fun. He just had to be careful about how much he revealed. Jackie wasn't stupid, and she knew enough about him from their road trip that she could figure it out.

The first message was easy. He kept it simple, with a brief introduction and comments on her own profile. He tried not to get too personal. If he could steer away from details such as profession and hobbies, he might be okay. But he knew it was a long shot. He just couldn't ask her the questions himself – not that he needed to.

Her reply back was equally brief, but polite. She of course asked the stand-by questions: what do you do for a living? What do you do for fun? How long have you lived in the area?

Okay, maybe this was going to be harder than he thought it would. He would have to try and keep it light, upbeat. He could do that. How could he avoid the dreaded questions? What could they talk about? The weather? Was there anything Jackie didn't know about him? Hmm...

He decided to discuss his work with the Chamber of Commerce. She didn't know he had joined, so that should be safe. He enjoyed spending time outside – true enough, and another topic that he was pretty sure had never come up, since they had spent most of their time together in the late fall and winter. And he would tell her he had grown up in the area, which was true. Yes, he had moved away when he was in his teens, only to return last year, but she didn't need to know that right now. And at least he wouldn't be lying to her.

Paul's heart was racing. He had thought it would be so simple, so easy, but here he was, sweating like a pig. He was ready to throw the towel in already, and they had barely said "hello." This would never work.

His hands were poised above the keyboard, ready to explain who he was and why he was doing this, when he stopped. This was important to him. He wanted Jackie to get to know him. And not the superficial things they would discuss in the first date, but the real substance below that. And he wanted her to give him a chance. He was afraid that if they met up next month, even with the intention of starting fresh, that the past would taint her view of him. He would forever be the person who kissed her too soon. She would see him as being on the rebound, not over Pam, not ready to be in a real relationship. But the past few months had been eye-opening for him. And he had to show her the real him, not the pre-judged version.

So he answered her questions as he had decided to and then took a chance.

Jackie was pleased to find a message from Andrew waiting for her when she logged on the following day. He had been her most promising lead since Adam, and she hoped things would work out. His message, however, was not quite what she expected.

He answered her questions, albeit briefly. But once they were answered, he made a proposition: that they skip all the meaningless chitchat that didn't teach you anything about a person and instead discussed what really mattered. He suggested life choices. Kids. World views. Perhaps politics, though that could get sticky. What was really important to them.

Jackie paused, unsure what to make of it. Was it an attempt to keep her from knowing about him? Or was it truly a way to learn the important stuff rather than waste their time with banalities? She supposed it could be both, but she wondered why someone looking for a life partner on a dating site would shy away from sharing personal information. And she knew he was looking for a life partner – it indicated on his profile he was interested in marriage and kids. The profile didn't divulge much more, but it did say that. So maybe this really was a way to cut to the chase. After all, was it really worth it to waste time with questions that would come out eventually anyway? Did you really learn anything about someone that way?

She decided to take a chance. Okay, they were going to talk about the meaningful stuff. What was important to her? Thinking about her volunteer work and upcoming education, she decided to start with giving back to the community. If he thought it was a waste of time, well, then, he wouldn't waste anymore of her time. If he agreed that it was important, then perhaps they would have something to start with. She sent it out into cyberspace, then stood up to get a snack.

Sipping a cup of tea and breaking apart a piece of pound cake, Jackie mused that Andrew hadn't said anything about meeting in person. Usually the people she met online were anxious to get together in real life. Perhaps he wanted to see if they were compatible first.

He seemed interested in the person inside, as opposed to outward appearances. The surface questions were one sign, as was the fact that he hadn't posted a picture. Then again, that could be because he was not an attractive man and didn't want to meet someone until he was sure they liked him for who he really was. Though posting a picture could perhaps better ensure that someone was willing to accept his appearance.

It was interesting how much time she had spent thinking about this man she didn't know. Perhaps that had been his intent: throw her off with unusual requests to peak her curiosity, to reel her in. If so, it was working. Now she just had to see what he would say next.

The month flew by, wrapped up as they both were with work and volunteering. Jackie began to look forward to her conversations with Andrew at the end of a busy day. She had grown quite fond of him, and with each day that passed, the anticipation of getting to speak to him grew.

They had discussed meeting, but so far they were unable to get their schedules to coincide. Jackie was afraid it was a bad omen, but he seemed so perfect for her that she didn't want to read too much into it.

In the middle of June, Andrew sent her a message suggesting that coming Friday to finally meet. Based on their discussions, he had deduced that Fridays were a good day for her, and he had an unexpected evening off. Jackie jumped at the chance and replied with an acceptance. It wasn't until she went to put the date in her beautiful leather datebook that she saw the big red letters and remembered her date with Paul.

Jackie leaned back in her chair and stared at the datebook. Wow. She hadn't thought about Paul in a while. It was surprising, really, considering how much time she had spent thinking about him at the end of the previous year. How could she have forgotten their important meeting? This was to be their fresh start, their new beginning. How could she tell him she had forgotten? That she would need to reschedule? And yet how could she reschedule on Andrew, when they finally had a chance to meet in person? Was she willing to give up a chance to meet the man who could be the love of her life?

Perhaps she could do both. She and Paul hadn't set a time, nor had she and Andrew. Perhaps she could meet Paul in the afternoon, and Andrew later in the evening. She and Paul were just supposed to have coffee, after all. She imagined her date with Andrew would involve dinner.

Of course, for this all to work she would need to call Paul and set a time. She was surprised he hadn't already given her one, to be honest. He had planned it all out, and yet he had left it open-ended. Reaching for her cell phone, she decided to call him now, before she forgot or chickened out. It shouldn't be a difficult call. This was Paul, after all.

He answered after two rings. "Hello?"

"Hi, Paul. It's Jackie."

"Jackie! How are you?"

"I'm great. How are you?"

They caught up a bit before Jackie touched on the initial reason for the call. "We never set a time for Friday. Did you still want to get together?"

"Wow. I can't believe it's here already."

Jackie smiled. "I know. Time flies. If you're still free, I was thinking afternoon? After the office closes? I can meet you at the office if you'd like."

"That would work. We can walk over to that cafe down the street."

"Sounds good. I'll see you then."

"See you then. I look forward to it."

"Me, too." Jackie was still smiling when she hung up the phone. It would be good to see Paul. Hearing his voice brought back fond memories. It seemed like forever since they had seen each other, but they had picked up right where they had left off. She didn't know how much of a fresh start this would be, but it would be good to see him, at least. And the office closed at three, giving her plenty of time to make plans with Andrew for the evening.

Chapter 29

Paul was nervous. Today was the day, and he was both excited and terrified. He had no idea how Jackie would react to finding out Andrew was in fact Paul. Would she feel betrayed? Excited? Confused? Angry? He was pretty sure they had grown close over the past month. She seemed to open up to him, and their conversations had grown increasingly personal, affectionate, and long. He was amazed at how much they had in common, but there had been enough differences to spark lively debate and conversation on a regular basis. He looked forward to talking to her at the end of each day. He pictured her sitting across from him, eyes twinkling, lips curved up in a smile. If this wasn't love, he didn't know what was. Now he had to take the chance that she wouldn't leave him completely when he came clean. But it was a chance he had to take. And considering one possible result was that he and Jackie could be together, it was a chance he was more than willing to take.

Jackie had butterflies in her stomach as she got ready to meet Paul. It was strange, meeting two men in the same day. It wasn't like her at all. Not that her meeting with Paul was really a date, but it felt like one. They had had a connection, and having coffee with him didn't feel like just having coffee with a friend. It felt like more.

But she really liked Andrew, and she didn't want Paul to affect her relationship with him. She would have to put each man out of her mind when she was with the other. It would be difficult to say the least. She was bound to make comparisons. She could only hope she didn't find Andrew lacking when compared to Paul. She would definitely be disappointed if her mind began playing those tricks on her. Andrew seemed like a good man, and he deserved to be given a fair shot.

It felt strange walking into the office where she used to work. The ladies in the office greeted her warmly, and they chatted a bit while Paul finished up with his last patient of the day. Seeing the waiting room, the desk, the file cabinets, it was hard to picture herself there. Yet she had spent ten years in that office, answering phones and helping patients. She had been happy there, if somewhat unfulfilled. Just a year ago she couldn't have imagined herself anywhere else. And yet here she was, her life a far cry from what it used to be.

Paul had made some changes to the office, and they discussed those changes while they had their coffee. Paul seemed nervous, which was strange, given his warm greeting and affectionate embrace. Perhaps he was reflecting her own tension. Being with Paul, talking to him, seeing his smiling face, she could remember Boston and their road trip. She could remember the frantic drive back to see Dr. Collins in the hospital. She could remember the awkwardness before she left, the almost hostile conversations afterward. And she could remember Christmas, and the simple joy of delivering gifts to those in need. She had a history with this man, strange as it seemed. They hadn't known each other long, but their lives were intertwined now, driven as they both had been to change themselves and figure out what they wanted out of life.

It would be difficult meeting Andrew after having coffee with Paul. She should have scheduled it for a different day. And yet how could she have? If they hadn't met today, who knew when they would be able to meet. It had been a headache already. But sitting here with Paul, maybe it wouldn't have been such a bad thing. Maybe she should have met with Paul before making such a choice.

"So Jackie, I'm sure I've bored you thoroughly with this talk of mural painting and new file systems. What have you been up to?"

It took her a moment for the question to sink in. She attempted a smile. "Well, I got into college. I start in the fall."

"Congratulations. Still going for social work?"

Jackie nodded. "Yeah. The more I volunteer the more I realize it's what I want to do. I love helping people."

"That's great. I take it you're still volunteering, then."

"Yup. The soup kitchen actually hired me as office manager, so part of it is paid, but I still help out with the kitchen periodically, and I spend a couple of hours a week at the social services department, too. Things are kind of quiet there this time of year, but they still need help in the food pantry and such."

"I commend your dedication."

Jackie blushed. "Thanks. So what else have you been up to?"

"Oh, this and that. I'm working with the EDC on the farmer's market. It goes throughout the summer, so that's been keeping me busy. And I've been attending chamber of commerce meetings, so that fills up some time, too."

"You've been busy."

Paul nodded. "That I have. But I enjoy it. I never realized how much I would love planning and organizing and all that. Pam always took charge of that kind of thing when we were married, so I never had the opportunity. But it's fun. And I feel like I'm contributing, which is nice."

Silence fell, and it was a slightly uncomfortable silence. Jackie didn't know what to say. Had they exhausted all topics of conversation? That was disappointing. Grasping for straws, she asked about Pam. "Have you talked to her lately?"

"We get together periodically, kind of like what we're doing now. The divorce was final back in March, but we've found we're capable of being friends. Surprisingly there isn't any tension there. We can talk about pretty much anything."

"Do you miss her?"

Paul paused a moment, as though contemplating the question. "I miss not being alone. It would be nice to have someone to come home to. But Pam and I weren't compatible as husband and wife. It took me a long time to see it, but it's true. We're better as friends. I'm glad we can still have that."

"I'm glad you found something that works."

"Me, too. The hardest part about the divorce was having to give up on our shared history. It wasn't even feeling like I was losing the love of my life. It was just turning my back on who I had been for ten years. Now I don't have to. I feel like I've just reached a different stage in my life."

"So you're happy?"

"Somewhat. Are you?"

"I'm getting there." She smiled.

"What would make your life perfect?"

"Hmm." She thought for a moment. "My career seems to be heading in the right direction, so I'm good on that front. I enjoy my volunteer work. I guess it's just what you said: having someone to come home to. I would like to be married, have children. I feel like that part of me is missing."

"Are you seeing anyone?"

"I was dating a man named Adam for a little while, but there was no chemistry. We broke up in April. I'm talking to someone now, but I can't say I've been seeing him since we haven't met yet."

Paul leaned forward. "Are you going to meet him?"

Jackie blushed again. "I actually have plans to meet him tonight."

"Oh, really? That's a shame. I was going to see if you wanted to do dinner or something."

"I'm sorry. Perhaps another time?"

"I'd like that." He smiled at her and put one hand over hers.

They lingered for a bit before Jackie told him she needed to go. They made plans to get together the following week. Paul suggested making Friday afternoons their time to get together. Jackie agreed, but she wasn't sure what to think about it. Depending on how things went with Andrew, she could see herself becoming torn. She was already starting to feel things for Paul that she had hoped had gone away. And she was already starting to feel things for Andrew that would make things awkward with Paul.

But she liked Paul, and she had no reason to refuse him. So she would look forward to seeing him until she had a reason not to.

She had about an hour before she had to meet Andrew, so she swung home to freshen up. Though she had started to relax in Paul's company, her butterflies had returned, and she wanted to make a good impression.

He had said he would be wearing a baseball cap, though they had arranged to meet at a reasonably-fancy restaurant. She supposed it would be easy enough to spot him. She only hoped she wouldn't make a fool of herself. As she stepped into the restaurant, she took a look around and, seeing no baseball caps, opted to wait at the bar rather than stand around like a lost puppy. She ordered a cola and had just taken a sip when she heard a voice behind her.

"You must be Jackie."

She turned to find Paul standing by her stool, removing a baseball cap and handing her a rose.

The look on her face was priceless. Surprise, followed by confusion, followed by a questioning look that lingered.

"Paul? What are you doing here?"

He took a deep breath. Damn it, he was nervous! "I came to meet you."

"But…" Her voice tapered off as she began to get an inkling of what might be happening. "I'm supposed to meet…"

"Andrew."

"Yeah. How did you…?"

"Andrew is my middle name."

"You're…?"

"Yes."

"But…Why?"

"Why don't we get a table and talk? I know you probably have lots of questions, and I'd love to answer them all. But I'd rather not give the bartender a story to tell."

She followed him up to the maitre'd, then to the table they were assigned. He could only imagine what she was thinking, how she was feeling. As for himself, he was running through just about every emotion possible. Would she accept him?

She looked beautiful sitting across from him. She had gotten dressed up for the occasion, and the royal blue dress suited her. His only complaint would be that she looked stiff, awkward, as she struggled with confusion. He had known it would be difficult for her, but he hoped they could move past that.

She waited until after they had ordered their meals before she spoke. "So you're Andrew."

"Yes."

"And you found me online because...?"

Paul took a deep breath. He had prepared an explanation, but it didn't seem enough. "Because I wanted to get to know you without the awkwardness that we had before. I know we had some ups and downs, and I was afraid that when we met up again we would let that take over. I want to have a fair shot with you. I like you, Jackie. I have from the beginning, but it didn't really hit me until a month ago how much."

"So you pretended to be somebody else."

He shook his head. This would be the most difficult to explain away. "No. I was myself. Except for the name, everything I told you was true. Our conversations, our bantering, our debates – it was all me. It would have defeated the purpose if I lied."

She was silent for a moment. He could see the emotions flickering across her face.

"I know it may not make sense, but I hope you'll give me a chance. If you had any feelings at all for Andrew, give me a chance."

"It's a lot to take in, Paul. I may not have had a picture of Andrew, but I had an idea of what he looked like. I had visions in my head on how this meeting would go. To have to transfer all the conversations of the past month to you is a bit of an undertaking. It changes my perception of everything."

"But it doesn't have to. Think about our conversations on our road trip. Were they really that different? We had that same connection."

He could see her processing. Her eyes looked far away as she sat deep in thought. What was she thinking behind those beautiful eyes?

Of all the crazy schemes. What had he been thinking, tricking her like that? What game was he trying to play?

And yet she did what he asked. She thought about her conversations with Paul and her conversations with Andrew. Knowing the truth she could see a lot of similarities. She could accept that they were the same person. But why lie about it?

He had said he wanted to give them a fair chance, to get to know her without the awkwardness. She could understand that.

So did that mean she was accepting this? That she was accepting him? Both of him?

"I can't say we're meant to be, Jackie. I honestly don't know. But I like you. I think we could be good together."

He was talking, but she was still thinking.

"You know, I didn't get to finish my road trip. *We* didn't get to finish our road trip. It wouldn't be the same without you. Nothing seems the same without you, but we can start with that. What do you say?"

Jackie paused as she gnawed her lower lip. The road trip? Now he wanted to finish the road trip? After the ups and downs, the uncertainty and decisions, was this what she wanted? Did she want to take this chance? Would she live to regret it? Would she live to regret not taking it? "I start school in the fall." It was the only thing she was sure of.

"We'll be back in plenty of time."

"I don't know if I can afford it anymore."

"We'll stick to a budget. Pretend we're college kids on a shoestring." He grinned, but Jackie could see the hope in his eyes – and the uncertainty. He was afraid she'd say no. Would he go without her?

"If I say no, would you still go?"

Paul sucked in a breath. "Yes. I'm determined to finish what I started. I still want to experience it. But it would be a whole lot more fun with you by my side."

"Is that why you did this? To get me to go on your road trip?"

"No. I did this because I wanted to have a chance with you."

"Then why the road trip?"

"Because it's unfinished business. For both of us. And I think it's important to finish what I started. So I can move forward. So *we* can move forward."

Finish what I started. The words echoed in Jackie's ears. She hadn't finished it either. And this new Jackie, the more assertive, confident Jackie, wanted to see it through to the end. Was she going to let the fear and timidity of the old Jackie ruin that for her? "Okay."

Paul grinned again. "Okay?"

Jackie nodded and returned the smile. She didn't know if it was the right choice, but after all they'd been through, how could she not find out? "Okay."

Paul hugged her suddenly then, and Jackie could only laugh. "We're gonna have so much fun, Jackie. Just you wait."

"We shall see. So when do we leave?"

Epilogue

"**H**ere you go, Noah. Why don't you put the last ornament up?"

Paul handed the child the glass ball, then stepped back and put an arm around Jackie's shoulders. His heart swelled with pride as he watched the four-year-old tuck the ornament among the tree branches.

"Can you believe it?" Jackie rested her head on Paul's shoulder. She didn't have to elaborate for him to know exactly what she was talking about.

It had been a year since they had gotten married in a small, simple ceremony – just six months after finishing their road trip. They had talked about everything on that trip, but the one thing they had both been most passionate about had been their desire to have a family.

Neither was getting any younger, and they made the decision that if things worked out between them, they would look into adopting. Two weeks after their wedding they were talking to the Department of Children and Families. They opted to become foster parents, with the understanding that they would be matched with children who had a greater chance of needing forever homes.

Noah had been with them three months when the word came that he was up for adoption. The paperwork should be finalized by Christmas. Paul couldn't think of a greater gift.

Thinking back on all that had happened, he couldn't believe any of it. He looked around at his inherited house, and he felt Uncle Bill's presence. He knew Bill would be proud – thrilled – to watch Paul and Jackie building a life together in this old house, raising a family, living the lives they were meant to live. And as he looked into his wife's shining eyes, Paul couldn't be happier.

www.ingramcontent.com/pod-product-compliance
Lightning Source LLC
Chambersburg PA
CBHW060416310726
48976CB00003B/1078